Prime Mincer

1.1

Spring 2011

Subscriptions: $27 for 1 year (3 issues). Inquire for international and institutional rates.

Submissions are accepted year round.

For more info regarding subscriptions, submissions, general rants, raves or anything else, please visit the website.

www.primemincer.com

ISBN-13: 978-0615459318
ISSN-10: 0615459315

Cover Photography by Eric Robinson.

Prime Mincer is Peter Lucas, Abigail Wheetley and Amy Graziano. However, this issue could not have come together as well as it has without the help of Sequoia Nagamatsu and Allison Joseph. Also, as always, we would like to thank Dexter Wheetley, Emily Wheetley and Jacob Lucas. You kids rock

CONTENTS

Sincerely

June 3

Eleanor:

I was relieved to receive your postcard today. You seem to find this difficult to remember, but I am both personally and—less important, perhaps, but nevertheless the case—legally concerned with you. As you know, the terms of your father's will make me your guardian until you turn twenty-one. Thus there are slightly less than four years remaining in which you are obligated—though I hope it's not such a heavy burden as all that—to keep me posted on what you are doing.

But I see that this letter is already off to a bad start. I had not intended to hector you and that, rereading reveals, is exactly what I have been doing. Forgive me for worrying, in my excessive and old-fashioned way, about a young girl on her own in the United States, a country about which one reads the most horrible things.

And let me begin again.

It was just after your parents' accident, six years ago, that you last visited Japan. You were here, I recall, in mid-August and—as your father and mother had when they visited a year or two before you were born—you found the heat and humidity unbearable. Granted, it can be trying, but as you may recall, I have determined that living without air-conditioning helps one accustom oneself to it. That's what I have done these thirty years and I seem, even at my age to survive the heat and humidity better than most of the youths I see passing my window, mopping at their foreheads with rags and handkerchiefs.

But again, I seem to be getting off on the wrong track. What I had meant to say is that early-June in Japan is nothing like the mid-August inferno that you may imagine you remember. It is sunny, bright, and warm but not too hot, too sticky, for even the most delicate among us to stroll the neighborhood and admire the flowers and plants to which my neighbors devote so much of their time and all of the garden space they haven't already surrendered to their cars. Thus I encourage you not to tarry in the States but to come as quickly as you can to me here in Chigasaki. I have aired the futon and have arranged a space for you in my work room. I'm sure you would enjoy your stay here provided you arrive before the real heat and humidity sets in, climactic conditions which, as I've mentioned, your side of the family has always affected to deplore.

(Remember, I am just a fifteen-minute walk from the beach, and though they nag one these days about the dangers of sunbathing I seldom missed a day of summer sun when I was younger and it hasn't harmed me in the least. Quite the contrary, I believe.)

If you have yet to make your plane reservation I encourage you to do so immediately. As you know, tickets can be hard to come by at the beginning of summer vacation what with legions of backpack-toting youngsters off to "do" Europe and South-East Asia. Economy-class tickets can be particularly scarce, and though your parents left a decent sum, still, business-class tickets are over-priced. Therefore I trust it will be an economy ticket for which you will compete with the backpacking horde. I have certainly never felt the need—or had the wherewithal— to fly anything other than economy.

Mrs. Sato, my eighty-six year old neighbor remembers you. Do you recall how, at age eleven, you convinced yourself she was a witch? Granted, she is not a beautiful woman, wasn't at eighty and probably not ever . . . but a witch! How did you get that into your head—the dark kimono, the wispy gray hair, the constant cigarette, that ghastly laugh of hers? In any case, I told her I expected you soon. She says she's eager to see you.

She's eager to see you, and so am I, as you've not visited since you began your time at that rich girls' school to which I was compelled to send you in spite of the outrageous fees. (Your father and I both attended public schools, and both of us—he in the blustery world of business, I as a literary translator, were successful.) As the lawyers who handled your parents' estate and still look after your affairs had the cheek to remind me, it wasn't my money but my brother's—your father's—I was fussing about, and now that he was dead, all of it was for your maintenance. (You understand that for all that I do toward supervising your upbringing, for keeping an eye on the lawyers who keep an eye on your money, I am not, and have never asked to be, compensated [recompense for expenses such as your keep when you finally arrive here in Japan, of course, excepted].)

And, remembering my desire to write you a letter free of complaints, allow me simply to ask, as your card is postmarked San Francisco, what it is you are doing in that provincial burg (a dreadful place, though finding amusement where one may, one does love to watch the locals cringe as one mouths the forbidden syllables: "Frisco"). You don't explain—there isn't, to be sure, room on the card to do so—what it is that has taken you there. The picture of the cable-car coupled with your cryptic comment "SCHOOLS OUT" don't go very far toward elucidating the situation. I will look for a letter from you explaining, and also discussing the decisions you have made about your future now that you have graduated from that dreadful finishing school. Or better, a note announcing your immanent arrival. I know it sounds archaic, but as I still have no phone and have no plans to acquire what you call "email"—shouldn't it be e-mail?—, if you need to reach me in a hurry a telegram is the most reliable method.

But again, I find myself drifting into schoolmarmish hectoring, so I'd best stop here.

Uncle Paul.

P.S. You sign your postcard "El." As there was space to have written your full name I'm not sure what motivated you to abbreviate it. As concerned with the rhythms and beauties of language as I am, I cannot believe that you have chosen this moniker over the more euphonious name which my brother had the uncharacteristic good taste to bestow on you.

———

June 29

Eleanor:

Mexico!

Imagine my surprise to receive a letter—that it was a letter and not an ugly little card was startling enough—from you postmarked San Miguel de Allende. This is the first I've heard you mention Paulie; is she (he?) a friend from school? In any event, I suppose we must be grateful to her—and especially to her grandfather—for inviting you to stay.

You say you have no idea how long you'll be there. Surely you've picked up some notion of how long you'd be welcome, and though you're distressingly vague about your future, I assume your decision to enter university in September is firm. Did you go ahead and apply to U.C. Santa Cruz? As you know, if you go to university your education and living expenses—and a good deal more—will be paid, but if you choose not to attend school the funds will simply remain buried in the trust beyond your reach, indeed beyond the reach of anyone who might have a claim on them. Your father, I hardly need add, botched the job terribly when he set up that trust. His incompetence in this matter is surprising, I suppose, since he is usually thought to have possessed that mysterious quality I have seen referred to as "business acumen."

And how are you finding Mexico and San Miguel? It's been years since I was there, years, frankly, since I've had money enough to leave the archipelago at all, but when I was younger and—I never had any money then either—capable of a more rough and ready style of travel I spent the odd summer in Guadalajara, in Cuernavaca, and, yes, in San Miguel. In fact it was my chronic lack of funds that drove me south of the border, that and the not inconsiderable attraction of a culture so close to the U.S. geographically but so far from America in every other respect. You will recall, perhaps, from your earliest years, that I never joined your family at the house on Martha's Vineyard. It's true, I was never asked, but who would want to summer anyway among the vulgarians who frequent that overrated bit of real estate anyway? (And I'm sure you will understand that my use of the word "summer" as though it were a verb is ironic.)

In any case, it was in Mexico that I began my career—I didn't realize at the time that it would become a career—as a translator. Though I really had nothing beyond high school Spanish and a passion for literature (the passion is still there, the Spanish is long gone) I managed, thanks to the odd contact made in a bar, a cafe, a plaza, and to the proud and fallacious letters I sent out, to convince folks that I was a literary translator. Indeed it was one of those braggadocios letters that convinced Julio Cortázar—he was living in Mexico City then—to send me a story. I translated it—with a great deal of his help; his English was better than my Spanish—and it made it into several anthologies—something about a lizard as I recall—and I was launched. I had become the literary translator I had once pretended to be.

In fact it was in San Miguel that I began to study Japanese too, but that's another story we'll leave for another time, for a conversation, I hope, rather than a letter. I imagine you'll tire of Mexico in a month or so and will then be ready to join me here in Nippon. You'll find that rather than flying directly to Japan from Mexico City you'll save a good deal of money if you change planes in Los Angeles, and at your age the lay-over should be no problem.

Rereading the above I wonder if it was wise of me to have regaled you with stories about my misspent youth. Please don't make the mistake of thinking that just because I've never been to university—

5

we won't mention the one quarter I attempted at Berkeley—you needn't go either. Times have changed, and you haven't—I must be frank—given any evidence of the sort of focus I had at your age. Further, as I have mentioned, you would, in foregoing education, do yourself out of a good deal of money, money you wouldn't see until you were twenty-one. As you have never, to my knowledge, worked a day in your life that is not something to take lightly.

Remember too that if you come to Japan we can apply to the estate for your fare and other travel expenses including room and board while you are here. I'm sure you know how to contact that awful lawyer—I imagine you can do so by e-mail!—and as staying with me is free we might just be able to turn a tidy profit on the deal.

Do write as soon as you can and let me know when I can expect you.

Paul

P.S. You mention that your friend's grandfather is a photographer. I can't imagine any of my old crowd is still around but as a grandfather of one of your contemporaries would, I imagine, be about the right age I must ask: what's his name?

———

July 6

Eleanor:

Our letters, it appears, crossed in the mail. I see that the slower pace of life in Mexico—I imagine you penning your missive in one of the cafes on the plaza in San Miguel just as I used to do—has allowed you the focus you need to write actual paper-and-pen letters. (You tell me that there are now at least four "internet cafes" in San Miguel. I have little idea what this tidbit is meant to convey and even less of a notion of what I'm supposed to do with it.) I say that the slower pace of Mexico must have allowed you to concentrate enough to write a letter, but then, on second thought, I wonder if you were in some way harried. Surely the, shall we say, impressionistic grammar and usage which characterize your letter is not what they taught you at the highly-touted East Coast establishment you attended? ("Unique" means one of a kind. Thus your no doubt charming friend Paulie either is unique or is not. She cannot be "extremely unique.")

I was happy to find that you are staying with my old friend Jerry Marston. When he was a much younger man he styled himself "Jerzy Modigliani" if you can believe that. Americans, you see, were *declassé* in our set, and he was trying, in this unlikely melding of a Polish name with an Italian one to suggest that he was European. That sounds rather silly, but still, one does understand what—Norman Mailer was widely believed in America at that time to be an important writer—might give one cause to do something as ludicrous as call oneself Jerzy Modigliani. Do mention my name to him—though I doubt he'll remember me.

But I go on too long about myself. I want to hear more about your life in Mexico, about the students with whom you are spending time. (What exactly does it mean for one to major in "healing"?)

And, as you tell me that Marston is doing well now and seems happy to have you there I suppose there is no particular reason why you should hurry to Japan. In fact, reading your descriptions of Mexico—the light, the fruit arranged in multicolored pyramids in the market, the life of the plaza—makes me, who gave up traveling years ago, eager to be there with you. Unfortunately, though it would hardly be missed from my brother's estate, I am certain the lawyers would never allow a dime of my brother's money out of their grasping hands even for such a worthy cause as bringing us, the last two surviving members of the family, together in such a delightful spot.

Of course they are much more amenable, I have learned, to your requests for money than they are to mine. That trip you suddenly decided you had to take to Nepal, of all places, after your junior year, for example, must certainly have been financed by them, or rather by the pile of your father's money that fell into their hands. (Interestingly,

7

I've begun to see the padlock that your father claimed to have invented, and on which his fortune was built, here in Japan. This suggests that his business is still a going concern and that the lawyers must still be raking in the dollars.)

Well, if there were any way for me to return to Mexico I would, but as I survive, for the most part, on the pittance my translations bring me that doesn't appear to be in the cards. In any case, do mention to Marston that I would love to see him once again in San Miguel. I even suspect my long dormant Spanish might rise to the surface if I had the opportunity to spend some time in such a congenial environment. Perhaps with a bit of practice I could even follow your acquaintance Jorge as he explains "chakras" to me in Spanish. The preoccupations of your friends all sounds so different from the sort of "intellectual"—for so we took it to be—claptrap Jerry—or should I say Jerzy?—, myself, and others amused ourselves with in the cafes and cantinas of our youth.

Do write soon and let me know if I should expect you in Japan, and do remember that if there were any way I could join you in Mexico I would jump at the chance.

Paul

P.S. You ask whether Haut Brion (I assume that is what you mean by "Oat Brian") is a "good wine." My dear, it is one of the world's best, if not the best. Jerry must be doing very well indeed! What year was it?

———

July 17

Eleanor:

I have just received your postcard informing me, to my surprise, that you won't be attending university in Santa Cruz but that instead you will matriculate at something called the College of Integral Arts right there in San Miguel. (I note with regret that you have reverted to a postcard to impart this news, but I suppose I must thank you for using, this time, script small enough that even in the few inches provided you were able to convey a message more substantial than the two-word missives with which you have, at times, allowed yourself to be satisfied. Fortunately, though my eyes are not what they once were, I possess a magnifying glass of sufficient strength.)

I feel you must have known, when you wrote last, that you would be attending not Santa Cruz but this "College" in San Miguel. You forbore to mention it then, however, perhaps because you felt that I would in some way oppose your decision (as if my opposition has ever carried any weight with you or with the lawyers). True, I think your friend Paulie's decision to attend Yale is a wise one, and I am impressed that she will be doing so on a full academic scholarship. With your grades, however, the Ivy League is not an avenue open to you (though money would not have been a problem), so you must necessarily choose another path. Though this college you have found does not inspire confidence, still, as I have not forgotten the complete lack of support which I received when I left—when I was asked to leave—Berkeley, at a time when I very much craved the support of my parents and brother, you may find me more amenable to your choice than you had expected. (Am I right in assuming that the "integral arts" have some connection with the mysterious "chakras" you mentioned in your last letter?)

And the best news of all is that you are welcome to stay on indefinitely at Marston's place—it certainly sounds like he has enough room. (Peacocks roaming the garden! Taste was never one of "Jerzy's" strong points.) A word of advice: don't tell the lawyers that you will be staying there rent-free. Let them continue to pay into your account the money they suppose you will be using for your living expenses. That way you can build up a tidy little nest-egg for yourself, something which it is always prudent to do. Indeed I wish that I had been wiser that way when I was young, but then I didn't have your advantages, a fat trust to take care of me no matter what hare-brained move I might decide to make in my life.

Wishing I were there with you,

Sincerely,

Your Uncle Paul

————

July 17

Jerry:

Imagine my surprise upon receiving a letter from my niece Eleanor informing me that the schoolfriend's grandfather with whom she is staying—and who, it appears, is teaching her nightly to appreciate the ineffable qualities which make first-growths so sought-after, so expensive—is the same Jerry Marston with whom I shared a few fragments of my misspent youth. (I remember when you called yourself "Jerzy," and I, of course, was Paulo.) I am delighted to find that you are doing well, and felt I must write to congratulate you on your good fortune and also to thank you for your kindness in taking in my niece, first for a visit and then to live with you in what sounds like a very pleasant house while she pursues her education. From the little she has told me about it I imagine your place must be one of those lovely old houses with their verdant gardens in which we could never dream of living but to which we were occasionally invited by those few established writers and artists who would from time to time— slumming, one now realizes—condescend to join our group at the cafe. You are fortunate to now be, for so it appears, one of those older established artists yourself. (That you keep peacocks suggests that your garden is of a certain size!)

Me? I have nothing to complain of, I suppose. I am, as I am sure you are aware, a literary translator. (You will remember my youthful success which was also my entrée into the field: my translation of a story of Cortázar's which was included in a couple anthologies, won a couple of prizes.) Alas, translation, literary translation, hardly pays enough to keep the cat fed, particularly in a country as expensive as Japan, where I have resided these last thirty years, but somehow I get by. I lived in the great metropolis Tokyo for years, but prices and pollution finally drove me out to the suburbs, a beach-town called Chigasaki where I now reside in a small house with siding of—would you believe it?—brown cast-iron. Not exactly a palatial hacienda such as the one in which you are privileged to reside, but gracious enough and, in its simple, *wabi-sabi* sort of way, elegant. In any case it is ample for my needs. There is room for my desk, my dictionaries, a futon and a two burner stove on which I can make the coffee upon which I would largely subsist if it weren't for the old lady who resides next door—identical brown cast-iron house—and is pleased to make me presents of her very good Japanese home cooking. Widowed these last twenty-five years, children long since grown and moved away, she has yet to learn to cook for one.

I had initially hoped that Eleanor would be able to join me here in Japan this summer. We are the last two of our family—has she told you about her parents' accident?—and I understand that as she moves into adulthood and I into my dotage there will not be many more chances for us to meet. Indeed when I heard that she was in San Miguel, and then that she had found a home with you, I began to fantasize about how pleasant it would be to join the both of you there. Alas, I am far from having enough money to ever think about leaving Japan; Indeed I haven't done so in a decade. If there were any way I could make the trip, Jerzy, believe me, I would.

Do you recall the book we worked on years ago, that coffee-table book about Mexico's silver cities: their culture, architecture, food and whatnot. You'll remember that I did the text for it and you the photographs. It was with some pleasure that I came across a new Japanese edition of that book just last week when I made a foray into town to try to hustle some work. Your pictures are as stunning as ever. Looking at the book brought back to me how hard I had worked on it: it was the biggest project I had, up to that time, undertaken and I was proud of myself when I handed in a manuscript of 50,000 words. True, they shaved something like 49,000 of them off in the course of, as they called it, editing. How was one to know that what they wanted were merely captions for your pictures? Still, it was something of a shock to find that all I got out of it was the equivalent of US$250—and they even refused to put my name with yours on the cover. True, in those days one could get by for a while in Mexico on $250, but I must confess I was jealous of you, who, I know, made a better deal than I had, managing as you did to retain the rights to your photographs, and therefore to collect royalties. Indeed I imagine you still are collecting royalties on our book.

So it goes. Water under the bridge.

Keep an eye on Eleanor. She is, I imagine, a fundamentally good person (I haven't seen her for something like six years). She seems to possess that lumpish niceness that one associates with dogs and Americans. She does, however, appear unusually receptive to all the idiocies to which young people are susceptible nowadays. I guess, however, that one can't really hold the *zeitgeist* against her, can one? (Should I be concerned about this Jorge fellow?)

A glance at a few advertisements reveals that a flight from Tokyo to Mexico City (open return—there'd be no point in coming that far if I weren't going to stay a while) can be had for as little as ¥250,000 (business-class). I'll let you do the conversion. Of course that's for a direct flight. Going through L.A. or somewhere in Texas is, of course, cheaper, but at my age I couldn't take the lay-over.

And what on earth are the "integral arts?"

Yours,

Paul

P.S. Encourage Eleanor to write me. She is not the most faithful of correspondents.

———

July 18

Eleanor:

As you may know by the time you receive this I have written Jerry-Jerzy and reminded him of our old friendship—and also how, many years ago, he did me out of a good bit of money. Don't say anything to him about that. It's probably better for now that he assumes you are unaware of his shenanigans. I did, however, in my letter to him do my best to turn the knife of guilt and I believe if we work this right we can play on that guilt and also, if he hasn't changed in the years since I've seen him, on his essential niceness—Jerzy was always a pleasant oaf. I believe we can use that guilt to maneuver him into buying me a plane ticket to Mexico so I can join you there at his mansion. I am certain if you mention to him how happy you would be to see your last surviving relative there's a real chance he would go for it. Indeed from what you've told me it sounds like he has more money than he knows what to do with—Haut Brion with *Enchiladas Verdes* indeed!—so it wouldn't hurt him a bit to help out an old friend. If he balks all you'd have to do is mention your parents' accident, and how you were made an orphan at eleven. As he's the sort of delicate soul who refused, when I knew him, even to attend the bullfights—he claimed he "couldn't stand the cruelty"—yanking on his heartstrings should be effective.

I apologize for the brevity of this letter, but I want to mail it today so that we can put our plan into action as soon as possible. If you need to get in touch with me quickly Mrs. Sato has agreed to allow you to contact me at her number (81-467-55-3555). She doesn't speak English, but if you repeat my name often enough she should understand and will come and get me. (I'm sure Jerry won't even notice the cost of the call, but if you feel uncomfortable taking advantage of his generosity reimburse him out of the money which, I am sure, the lawyers are sending you for your "living expenses." Little do they know that Jerzy is already taking care of those.

Hoping to hear from you and "Jerzy" soon.

Eagerly,

Paul

_____

August 7

Eleanor:

Imagine my surprise, after hearing nothing for three weeks, to receive your post-card depicting the ruins of Machu Picchu. I am not quite the provincial you take me for; if, in referring to Machu Picchu as "one of the worlds (*sic*) seven powerspots (*sic*)" you are trying to make me understand the site's cultural importance you are telling me nothing I don't already know. As you impart little more than that commonplace in the inches allowed you on the back of the card I am at a loss to understand why you are in the Andes at all. I guess, as Jerzy—and his wallet—are with you, you aren't exactly roughing it, but still, how could you have turned your back on what sounds like such a lovely life in San Miguel especially when I was set to join you there for our family reunion.

Still, I suppose one mustn't pass up the chances that come one's way; if someone were to offer to pay my way to Peru I am certain I would jump at the chance just as eagerly as you did.

I wonder if Jerry is planning to arrange for my ticket upon your return—soon, I hope—to Mexico. Remind him once again that you and I are family—that I am the only family you have. That should do the trick.

Contact me as soon as you get back to San Miguel. In case you've mislaid Mrs. Sato's number it is 81-467-55-3555.

Awaiting word,

Paul

———

September 17

Eleanor:

The "invitation" to your wedding arrived—as I'm sure you knew it would—weeks late. Has Latin American honor really slipped so far that they will allow a couple consisting of a geriatric goat and a child to have their ceremony at an important archeological site? Apparently, if one has the kind of money that Jerzy has, it can be arranged. Frankly, the whole thing makes me sick—and the image you've conjured in your sloppy prose of you and Marston sitting among the ruins meditating— "absorbing," as you put it, "the power of the sun, the mountains, and the Inca Deities"—doesn't settle my stomach a bit.

Further adding to my bile are the cute extras you and Jerzy have included with the invitation. The crude caricature one of you has labeled "Beloved Uncle Paul" which sneaks along behind the two of you, one hand picking your pocket, the other picking his, is offensive—to say the least. I've told you enough about the way Marston has dealt with me that I'm sure you realize that he's the one who should be shown picking my pocket, not the other way around. That sticking out of the pants of the cartoon figure meant to be me is a manuscript labeled "Cortazar translation: Paul's moment of glory" is just silly.) The "humor" of the scrawled note—Is that Jerzy's writing?—asking after "my pretty Japanese boy" is opaque to me. One might as well ask after his "dumb rich girl." (And note that there is an accent over the first *a* in Cortázar.)

I'm certain you will find out what sort of man you have married soon enough, so there's no point in me telling you. I am, however, appalled that you have allowed yourself to join him in the crudity and attempted cruelty of his drawing and remarks. I would have thought the fact that I am the only remaining member of your family would have counted for something. Apparently it does not.

Of course when I heard about the marriage I immediately contacted the lawyers to see if anything could be done about it. With their usual rudeness they claimed there was not, informing me that upon your marriage, per the terms of the trust my bonehead brother set up, the entire estate passes out of their hands and into yours. They say that one of their professional brethren contacted them claiming to represent Mr. and Mrs. Marston and insisting that the Marstons wanted him to manage your estate along with the rest of Jerzy's holdings. Apparently, rather than looking out for our interests as one would have thought they were being paid to do, Jarndyce & Jarndyce acceded to this rather obvious bit of gold-digging on Marston's part. You'll just have to hope that he doesn't get all your money away from you and leave you penniless.

The other major change is that, of course, I am no longer your guardian. Though you have never expressed any gratitude for all I have done for you I believe you will one day come to understand the sacrifices I have made and regret the cavalier treatment to which you—like your father before you—have subjected me. The tone of your "wedding announcement" makes it impossible for me to offer you or Jerzy any further advice or assistance. Our relationship ends here. Now you will know what it feels like to be an orphan, and I'm sorry to say—sincerely sorry—that you won't find it pleasant.

Sincerely

Paul

———

October 23

Sr. Jorge Ruiz:

Your map reading skills are exemplary. Chigasaki is just a short way from Kamakura and, yes, there are Zen temples in that beautiful city. I was unaware that any of them accepted foreign aspirants, but I guess, since you tell me such is the case, that at least one of them must.

Your English is good, but, I am afraid, corrupted. I wonder if you picked up the rather gross locution "crash," as in your request "Would it be alright if I crashed at your place for a while?" from my niece. That's just the sort of solecism that I used to find in her rare letters. Indeed it is almost a relief that she has, apparently, given up corresponding with me altogether (though I am her only surviving relative). I no longer have to torture myself with the hash she makes of the English language.

Your manners, I am afraid, are not as good as your English. What ever gave you the notion that you could contact someone you don't know, and, on the basis of a passing acquaintance with a distant relative of that person, assume that you would be welcome to "crash" with him is entirely beyond my power to imagine. I'll put it down to a cultural difference—though I can't imagine any of my many Mexican friends behaving in this fashion.

As I do remember what it is to be young and starting out in a foreign country, however, I cannot resist offering my assistance. While it is not possible for you to stay with me, if you were to wire ¥100,000 or the equivalent in American dollars—not pesos!—I could probably arrange to have suitable accommodation ready for you upon your arrival. Indeed there is some chance a neighbor of mine, a widow in a house too big for her, might consider taking in a boarder.

The quicker you send the money the quicker I can get to work apartment hunting, so I hope to hear from you soon.

Sincerely,

Paul Hepford

P.S. I probably don't need to add that if you are able to send more than ¥100,000 that would make it possible to consider more luxurious accommodation.

It is Wide and It is Deep

The night before the raid I dream of Virginia. The sky is the soft blue and purple of my boyhood and I'm standing on the porch back on Dad's farm, looking out into the woods. There're shots and a rushing, someone out there running dogs, maybe treeing a coon or two. I know it's winter, but it's my dream and I'm able to make it just fine. I heat the air as easily as reaching for a thermostat and the whole world's a little warmer.

There's nothing but trees and shapes, but I know these woods like the rooms of my house and I take turn after turn, brush past the branches and move through. I keep reaching out toward the heart of it, the clearing in the middle where I know I'm heading. I've lived this moment a thousand times if I've lived it once.

When I get there I see Davey Hutchins, a short and angry man who walks with a terrible limp. The right side of his face is frozen in palsy and the corners of his lips sag toward his chin. He has a rifle, but it's tucked beneath his arm. One of his dogs, a bloodhound, squats at the base of a tree and points upward. Davey's squinting and trying to make something out.

It's a girl, he says. There's some kind of girl up there a howlin' and carryin' on.

A girl? I say.

Yep, Davey says. I'll be goddamned if there ain't some kind of girl up there.

I go and take a look for myself. It's dark, but looking up into the cradle of the branches, and against the light of a fat moon overhead, I'm able to see her soft curves. She's braced against one of the limbs with her head thrown back.

Davey scratches his chin and yells. You a girl? There a girl up in that tree? He sounds confused at first but his voice gets some sort of edge to it. He's shouting now. Come on down, he yells. Come on down or I'm gonna start shooting.

When she comes down it's easy to see she ain't got a stitch on her. Just as naked and free as anything you've ever seen. Long brown hair with knots and briars in it. Dried spit and dirt caked on her face. Big heavy breasts. She has a seat on the ground. Davey drops his rifle and mumbles something I don't catch. That bloodhound runs and hides behind his legs. The girl reaches up and paws at her cheek.

If it this ain't the best day of my life, Davey says, I don't know what was. Came out here looking for some coon or squirrel and got me a wife. Goddamn if this ain't the best day ever.

Before I can say anything he's lurching toward her and just about ready to have his way. The girl looks up at him and you can tell she's not real happy. She grimaces a little, bites her lip. Davey's already getting down in the grass with her, reaching to undo his belt and unzip his jeans. Before he gets down on his knees I pick up his gun and put the barrel to the back of his head and give him a little nudge.

Best be getting off that one, I say. Best just let her be.

You cocksucker, Davey says, not even turning around to face me. I don't know what you think you're doing, Harry, but you shouldn't be doing it.

I look past him and see the girl. She's all kinds of confused.

Turn around, I tell Davey. Turn right around here.

He does and I'm looking into that messed up mug of his. I trace the sad curve of his mouth with the barrel. He's so pissed he's starting to shake.

I say, If you don't want your pecker shot off you'll zip up.

In no time at all he's reaching down and putting himself away. He turns and I use the barrel to nudge him back to attention.

Now what you're going to do, I say, is get up and walk away from here. Got that?

Fuck you, he says.

No, I say, fuck you. Fuck you and get up and walk away. I'm not asking.

Davey doesn't move an inch.

Last time I say it, I say. Get up and leave and you never saw shit. Got it?

This time he doesn't even wait for me to finish. He takes off into the blackness of the wood, that blue tick trailing the whole way. I hear him limping through the brush and then nothing. I'm left with the girl.

I take off my coat and drape it around her. Already she's cooing and squirming to get in my arms. I take her and hold her close. I kiss her and it tastes like fresh-tilled earth. She's pulling me atop. Leaning back and spreading herself across the coat and the ground. I lower myself down onto her and thrust. I know she is my one and only.

*

The mess is mostly cleaned up before we get there. A cloud of smoke hangs heavy in the air and there are a dozen or so bodies burning in the sun, but the shots are in the distance now. Taped to the dashboard of the humvee is a picture of my one and only wearing a checkered top and she is sprawled across a blanket.

I get out and take me a look around. There's a row or two of captures over by the wall of a grocery store and they're lying on their stomachs with hoods over their heads. Some of their legs are kicking and their bodies flopping around. They look like catfish snapped ashore. A group of bored men stand watching from a distance, their hands in their pockets.

Eleven in all, my assistant says. Three more in the building. Got a team coming in to unload munitions.

How many we lose? I say.

Two, he says.

I say huh and wander over to the rows. There's a kid lying there, fifteen maybe, his hands bound behind his back and his hooded head thumping against the sidewalk. There's a wet stain dripping from inside his pants down to his knee. I put the point of my boot into his ribs and give a little shove. I say, Got a pissin' problem?

Our boys are huddled over by the caravan. They're taking a knee and got their weapons on the ground. They're tired and worn and one of them is holding his left hand with his right. Blood gushing down his wrist.

I'm so taken by the sight I start to tear up. If there's one thing I hate to see it's a soldier with a busted hand. Dad came home from Okinawa missing three fingers and never got over it. Sometimes I'd see him sitting there in his chair, looking over his mangled fist. It just about broke my heart to see anyone suffer like he did.

My assistant calls my name and steals me out of memory. He starts talking and points to one of the men lying face down in the road. All I hear are the words High Level and Priority.

*

In the basement, in a hallway past the bathrooms and the janitor's closet, is a room. In the room is a table and a sink. When I come in the fucker's already strapped in by his ankles and wrists. There's a belt

22

around his shoulders. Always a hood. Haven't ever seen a face and never care to.

There are two guards on either side and I tell them to fill the buckets. I straddle him and the table like I do my darling wife and, leaning down, I say, This had to happen. There are so few of you and so many of us. I am sorry you are weak.

A signal and the first of the buckets hits his face.

That is an ocean, I say.

Another comes down and his fingers claw at the table. His feet click together and there's a groan. Some words, but when I look at the translator he shrugs.

Do you know what ocean that is? Do you know what ocean you are drowning in?

Nothing but cries.

That's the American Ocean, son.

The translator tells me he has phone numbers. Addresses in Manchester.

And the American Ocean is wide.

A ledger in Pakistan. Notebooks with bank accounts.

And the American Ocean is deep.

A gurgle.

I say, The President's a good friend to have. He tells the water when to rise and when to fall.

Through his hood I stroke his face. Water seeps out of the cloth and I dip my fingers into its pools. I say, The President is a friend of mine. In the summer we clear brush and share iced teas on his porch while the massive sun sets over the Texan hills. You can hear the cattle bay in the evening breeze. He is a very good friend to have.

There is only crying now.

*

The doctor holds up cards with ink smeared across them. It bunches and forms arcs and splotches that look like things. Don't worry, he says. I mean, I understand I don't know quite what you've gone through over there. Not having been and all. We're here for you and as soon as we get this over with we can get those checks coming right along. Good? Good.

The first looks like a car and I tell him so.

And this? he says.

A house with a chimney, I say.

This?

A plate of steak and eggs.

He nods and shuffles the deck. One more, he says. One more and we can just talk for a bit. Get this whole thing over with. How about this?

There are ripples, as if someone had dropped a pebble into a sea of ink. They radiate out and toward the corners of the white card while the rock sinks.

There are ripples, I say. As if a pebble was dropped into a sea of ink.

Good, he says. He signs something and nods again. Very good.

*

My boys spring out of the house and rush down the drive to meet me. I've barely stepped out of the car before they tackle me and shower me with kisses. Their hair is parted perfectly and they wear tailored, tweed jackets. They are beautiful and they are my blood.

On the porch is my wife, wearing a yellow summer dress that barely contains her heaving chest. Her hair is loose and fanning over her shoulders.

You were missed every night of every day, she says.

I sweep her into my arms and press my lips against hers until neither of us still has breath. From there it is to the bedroom where she strips off my uniform in the proper order of jacket, tie, button down, slacks, and socks. She rubs fine oils over my back and chest and tells me when she is of the proper warmth and wetness.

*

A week in and I miss the feeling. I wait at the windows for caravans to come down the drive. While I walk the grounds I listen for the pop of rifles in the distance. I tell my wife and children to prepare for a hunt. We will leave at twenty-one hundred hours.

In the dark we walk off into the woods with our rifles. The dogs jet ahead while we trudge down through the ditches and the valley. The moon is high and full and once my eyes adjust I can see everything.

We wind through the trees and take a few shots at some squirrels, but end up empty handed. My youngest, Robert, swears the one he sighted was hit square and has to be bleeding out. So we follow him for a moment, his weapon slung across his back. At seven he is already blossoming into a man. He speaks his mind openly and does not tolerate foolishness.

A little ways south and the blue tick finds it ducked under a sticker bush. The animal is prone and dying. I try and tell Robert to be wary, but he gets down and crawls right in. Lee, my oldest son, follows his younger brother into the brush and they pull the squirrel out in the open. My heart beats and swells until it fills my chest. I pull my one and only tight and press my face into her nest of hair. When I inhale I can taste her perfume and it smells of lilac and spring mornings.

Look at these children, I say.

They turn and smile as if they'd heard my words. They prod the squirrel's trembling body with their guns and coo. Lee plucks hairs from its curled tail while Robert runs one young finger across its head, past the eyes and to its mouth. He pulls the jaw and when he lets it go it snaps back. It looks as if the animal is talking to us, chattering on about whatever, and we all lean forward, cupping our ears to try and listen.

Welcome, Psychotics!

Welcome, Psychotics!

to the long tunnel of hard voices
you carry inside your mind

while in the rest of country
Tea-Partiers storm the polls

like locusts or the fat and sassy
cockroaches of a post-nuclear

winter. Let them trip the trigger,
the voices say so strongly

it's as if there never was a choice
but to take a hacksaw to your shotgun

barrel and pull the plug too,
pack your family into a car

with four jerry-cans filled
with gasoline and false hope

as another someone speaks outside
your head about death being

the destroyer of worlds. Oppenheimer,
that's his name. The car jerks

its way up a short mountain in Sullivan
County PA not nearly far enough away

even with Death now narrating which turn
to take and for which you should engage

the wings of your aerocar and check
the weals on your skin beaten in

by mere air and stones. It's as if every god
that ever was has shared their golden

years in residence between your ears,
your only job to listen to them shout

and take action from what they say. Or not.

The Short Walk vs. The Long Lie

Sometimes walking the plank seems
the best option. Enter the watery main

where the fish kiss your face and you
whirl in a pool and fissure into tiny pieces

of flesh: blood to sea and back again
in something primordial like first sex:

all lines are drawn from zero where the marlin
tails its way into the spume sixty yards

ahead of the prow, and line-caught, it dives
again maybe six hundred years off the bow

Who can tell for sure? The sextant's handy,
cap'n, take her measure. Stem to stern this tub's

no goddess ship but it's what we have to steer
with. An artificial horizon is better than none

after all, nothing matters but this long plank
and that short walk, knowledge knocking

like waves on the side or a fired cannon recoiling
straight back into a deaf and dumb gunner.

That's quick though, not like the delicatessen in the waves
set for the regulars, shark and scavenger. Again you ready

for that walk into the long lie, salvation, where God
seems not to live anymore nor care if he does. As you

jump, watch for the marlin, the sparkle of his diadem,
his holy crown, that disappears even as it parts the waves.

Rusty Barnes

Between Nuclear Shadow and Salvation

The nuclear clock shows three minutes till, now.
Sometimes I think the post-apocalypse world

might be better than this one; no more of this
bullshit running around trying for a normal life:

have the kids/raise the kids/ watch television
until you sprout colitis wings and fly off dying

into the gangrenous ozone knowing you'll
never reach heaven or hell; they've reversed

directions on you, these religious advisers of yours.
And if you meet Jesus, the last thing he'll want to see

is the cross you've worn on your neck for twenty-
five years. It's off with the perverts and sycophants

with you. Better to float through the post-nuclear world
shotgun under your shoulder and children behind you,

needing protection, better to have a real world
and tangible nuke-zombies to fight against instead

of immanent salvation. Better to watch your wife
weep from her open wounds as she tries to feed

your latest soft-headed child with radioactive carrots,
landscape rotten with corpses and the dust of civilization.

The communal life you always wanted, angels with
malformed haloes all around you staring with rheumy

eyes, saying *cry with us* as you confront the formless
void. Even the carrot's half-life now is longer than yours.

Three About a Girl

Smitten

"Ice weasels are love," she said. "Fluffy pillows hate you." She was a strange girlfriend, I thought. She would hide around the corner of my apartment building and follow me to the market, trail me on public transport. She gave me a bag full of washers and scrap electrical wire for my birthday, saying that I might need it someday. I turn the wire into stick figures on my desk, the washers fit the washing machines when I'm shy a quarter. I wonder now where she went. She always talked about Russia, so maybe she is there, in Russia, evading kidnappers and savoring thin gruel.

Winter's Dim Light

She took her panties and put them in her purse. The coffee was almost ready, steamy-roast aroma filled the studio apartment and she stood, naked, in front of the window overlooking the city. I am sure people could see her there. I remembered being a teenager and wishing for such a neighbor, even one with small breasts and a port wine stain over half her torso. She enjoyed standing there in the draft of my cheap apartment, in the morning, before coffee, before toast, before the day.

It's Not Shakespeare

Only once did I have to stand up for her honor. We were in a pub to see one of her friends bang a sledgehammer onto an anvil while a montage of cartoon anvils flickered behind her. My girl was annoyed that her friend was doing it wrong and so she booed. A guy with a loose swagger doused her with a beer. So, I did my duty and I decked him. I knocked his tooth out and grabbed my girlfriend in movie-star fashion. She pushed me away and slapped me. "You are so off script," she said.

God and the Jack Russell

The Jack Russell bit the owner. *She's humongous and eats more food than I do. I want chicken breasts, not this lamb/rice shit. Okay, she mixes it with Parmesan cheese—big deal. Nothing tastes better than poultry parts dipped in succulent* schwartza[1]*-prepared barbecue sauce. That's one thing* schwartzas *are good at—barbecue sauce.* The owner sensed racism, and had read somewhere, perhaps on the Internet, that Jack Russells chased slaves who escaped Alabama plantations during the 1800s.

The owner was upset because cockroaches ate most of the lamb/rice, which cost her $25.99 a bag—on sale! She even contemplated using the methods of an ex-PETA activist who water boarded her cat for taking a dump in the laundry hamper.

The dog, with a black and white face and green/hazelnut eyes, stared at the neighborhood's trajectory of travelers that passed underneath the window. She looked dejectedly at the ceiling or played with decapitated toys.

They normally walked to Walgreens—and then a little further— after the owner joined the Lose Weight Club at work. They eventually traveled beyond the Walgreens garbage dumpster after the owner's doctor advised, "Stroll to prevent a stroke," but they rarely went around the block. This, of course, led to the Jack Russell bouncing/trouncing throughout their small apartment, causing indentations in the wall.

---

[1] "Schwartza" is a derogatory Yiddish term for African Americans.

The Jack Russell had a small Marmaduke that she received for her seventh birthday. She loved "Marmy," and she and the skinny brown toy pretended they were male canines dressed as bitches, also known as "dog queens." Marmy and her lover wore White Diamonds perfume and sniffed each other's butts.

But without good food and long walks the Jack Russell was depressed. This also led to negative revelations about her lover: *Marmy is not very sexy—he's too small and I do all the work. I'd prefer sex with Sweet Polly Purebred!*

The owner saw the dog's diminutive facial expressions and drooping eyes and caressed her teats. The owner surmised: I'll scratch her belly and go to work—where I administer grammar vaccines[2] to incompetent financial writers—and come home to dog kisses. What a life—words and tongues—she thought, as she opened the door to leave.

However, this day was different from others. The owner didn't turn the radio off and could not predict that the radio announcer would switch from jazz disc jockey to anti-homosexual Pentecostal minister.

The Jack Russell was always distressed by her owner's departure. She lowered her head, drank water from the bowl, and heard a deep and unhesitant voice resonate from the static channel: "The ruin that homosexuality is wreaking upon Native American Indians is devastating; these reservations are no longer conspicuously heterosexual and happy places. If we all pray, Jesus will destroy these infidels by sending them to Hades tomorrow morning. It is unthinkable for man to fornicate with man and woman to go downtown on woman. Would a Jack Russell have sex with a German shepherd?" he yelled to his disciples—the studio audience jubilantly responded, "Hell no!" This terrified the Jack Russell, who occasionally, when walking

---

[2] Contains .5 mL of *The Chicago Manual of Style*, with .2% alcohol-based words from E. B. White.

near Walgreens, sniffed a German shepherd who barked like a broken pencil sharpener.

The minister's voice blew through the Jack Russell's upturned ears. The little beast was soon consumed with Jesus and hedonistic German Shepherds and Native Americans who were victims of homosexual-manufactured crystal meth (cooked in high-end factories on broken floors in Albuquerque, New Mexico, that rested above cockroach-infested pizzerias, the Pentecostal leader declared).

The canine guiltily thought of Marmy. *This minister, who asks his followers to denounce gayness as some might oxygen, would not approve of dog queens.* "The Lord will not tolerate faggots or dykes!" Obviously, the animal felt, this must apply to canines and their synthetic lovers.

The dog, terrified by the speaker's rising decibels, reached for the headless blue/white teddy bear. She pushed the teddy bear and a red-haired Barbie doll together; she manipulated her toys into the shape of a cross. *If Jesus means anything to me, I must do this exercise and receive his blessings, which I do not get from Fatso. She starves me like an imprisoned member of the IRA. Her walks are equal to the length of a 4-inch treadmill.* (The Jack Russell detested the short strolls, but obsessively sniffed items in the Walgreens garbage dumpster, which became their destination point. Now and then she ate a chicken bone from the Islamic chicken store across the street that catered to cab drivers who did not permit either her or the owner to drink coffee in their café. The dog sometimes imagined that Arabs were African Americans and barked so loudly they spilled their Moroccan coffee.)

The Jack Russell shoved stuffed animals and one cotton boomerang into her crucifix sculpture—this made her relax; Jesus might forgive her for the sin of having sex with Marmy and lusting for Sweet Polly Purebred. *Marmy doesn't kiss well; when I reach for her tongue, I choke on cotton threads. And Sweet Polly Purebred is obsessed with a faggot named*

Underdog; her lust is like straight women throwing panties at Liberace in the sixties.[3]

The Jack Russell made her sacrifice to Jesus. She knew the owner was Jewish, but it was implausible to construct a Star of David—it was stressful enough to do this Toys R Us crucifix, let alone design a sculpture for the Chosen people. *No—this ain't happenin'*, she decided, *I have finally found the Lord and am going to achieve sirloin steak salvation in the afterlife.*

As the dog motioned (via snout) a beheaded Snoopy to the top of the crucifix, she heard the door open. It had been hours since the minister first frightened her into salvation (he still shouted from the portable radio). As she completed the crucifix, she heard Fatso open the door.

"What have you done to my living room?" The owner peered quizzically at the little canine, which stood proudly in front of her Pentecostal offerings. The owner had never seen a cross this large, let alone one that comprised her dog's entire toy collection.

She stared at the pile, where platypus met rhinoceros. There was a Dodo bird in the middle. Marmaduke, who normally maintained a position next to the canine's throne/bed, was at the bottom of the structure. Unlike Beatrice in Dante's *Divine Commedia* who reached heightened levels in *Paradiso*, Marmaduke was in the bowels of the *Inferno*.

The master listened to the evangelist's voice, "Either you give yourselves to Jesus or to a German shepherd."

This must be the correlation, the logic, the owner thought, which has brainwashed my dog into creating this disconcerting sculpture in our studio apartment. She turned off the radio.

---

[3] The Jack Russell was not alive during the sixties, but heard that when Liberace visited Durham, North Carolina, in 1962, the Daughters of the American Revolution organized a Fruit of the Loom collection.

The Jack Russell, who normally licked the owner, scarcely moved.

"Don't you want Marmaduke?" The owner disrupted the sculpture's permanence and removed Marmy, whom she placed next to the sneering Jack Russell.

"Are you anti-Marmaduke?" The Jack Russell continued to sneer, as if, on the Pentecostal minister's behalf, she might snap at this Jewish female.

"What you need," the owner quickly motioned to the leather leash hanging on the wall, "is a walk…." The walk word caused the Jack Russell to forget her newly acquired religiosity. She jumped toward the owner and aligned herself with the leather leash.

They went toward the Walgreens garbage dumpster. The Jack Russell enjoyed garbage although the owner feared such waste matter might corrode the canine's insides. Nonetheless, to the owner this was preferable to a mile-long stroll or the intersecting toys in the living room.

The small dog feasted on a selection of SPAM and frozen pizza crumbs. Her dexterity was such that she was able to ingest food before the owner could retrieve the unsavory smorgasbord from the dog's esophagus.

"Do you realize that SPAM is a culinary delight in Hawaii?" she asked the Jack Russell.

The Jack Russell barked, as if she and Jesus were finally at ease, and looked forward to future kissing sessions with Marmaduke.

Slices

Darkness drizzles over the city this evening before Thanksgiving. In his bright studio apartment's kitchen, Jesús Jimenez-Callaghan attacks pecans with a large knife. His drooping tangerine and turquoise boxers are smudged with flour. He chats with Carlos, who reclines on the adjacent Queen-sized bed. Carlos wears only a gingham apron and a chef's hat.

Jesús reads Betty Crocker's Sugar-Crusted Pecan Pie recipe aloud for a fifth time and then lifts a sample from each of the two piles he has hacked to pieces. The one in his left hand is miniscule; the right, bigger.

"Hey, Carlito, which of these would you say is chopped?" There is no answer. Jesús mixes both piles into one.

He believes that one day he will prepare a glorious meal and his family will be transformed by the dishes he has offered. Peace will settle over them like a flower picker's poncho in a Diego Rivera painting.

He does not see his inability to cook as an obstacle.

A few miles away his adoptive grandmother, Old Mrs. Callaghan, dices fresh flat leaf parsley for oyster stuffing, her Thanksgiving dinner specialty. The green scent of the herb reminds her of a time some twenty years earlier when Jesús refused to eat the corned beef and cabbage she had stewed all day for the family's Good Friday dinner. He was only five, and the powerful smell of that dish offended his naïve nose. He stubbornly shook his head side-to-side while Old Mrs. Callaghan just as stubbornly chased his mouth with a spoon.

"Take a bite."

"No."

"One little bite."

"No."

"You will sit here until you eat some."

Jesús scowled from the powder blue dinette chair for three hours, clutching his teddy bear in defiant little fingers. By the time a defeated Old Mrs. Callaghan dismissed him with a sweep of her hand, chick-a-dees and goldfinches had begun their twilight songs in the backyard roses. She dumped the coagulated food in the silver kitchen pail.

Later she watched as Jesús' mother fixed him packaged tortillas and canned refried beans.

Old Mrs. Callaghan vowed never to teach either to cook.

Colin Callaghan pours himself a whisky and watches his elderly mother dice the parsley. Something in the way she deftly turns the blade scares him, and when he is scared he tends to remember when his father died. Colin was two. His mother, he recollects, used to delight in telling Colin that his father had been found sprawled on the dining room floor.

"Like a boar laid out for skinning," she's told him over the years, pointing a harsh finger or a stirring spoon or, yes, a boning knife, "right there on the cold marble tiles." This information highly disturbed the fatherless boy. It still does.

Old Mrs. Callaghan also told Colin that directly after his father died she emptied two-and-a-half fifths of Irish whiskey down the toilet. Then she prayed.

MariaElena Jimenez-Callaghan picks through black beans. She will cook them in her special bean pot for the Thanksgiving dinner. She has sifted through beans so many times over the course of her 45 years that her fingers complete the task without thought, knowing by touch whether it's good bean or bad bean or rock. Her unencumbered mind reminisces about how she became a part of this family.

The twenty-year-old Mexican national learned she was pregnant with Jesús on a Saturday. That Monday, accompanied only by the fetus and the long shadow she cast in the midnight moonlight, she sprinted across a wide-open U.S. border. Once on the American side she didn't stop running until she landed in a maid's uniform in the Maryland suburbs of Washington. The baby's father, simple and fixated on doing what he'd been taught was right, and in love with MariaElena, followed her faint trail.

"*¿Quieres casarte conmigo?*" he proposed when he found her.

"Hell no," she answered. If she took a husband, he would be a citizenship-providing American with sufficient resources.

In a tequila-fueled attempt to prove his spousal worthiness, the rejected suitor robbed the SunTrust bank on DuPont Circle using a water pistol and broken English. He was sentenced four months later.

On the day of Jesús' birth he mailed a prison-commissary teddy bear, and two weeks after that, mistaken in a dark corridor for a different brown-skinned inmate, he was stabbed to death with the crudely-sharpened leg bone of a turkey.

As a Training Associate in the International University's Human Resources Department, Jesús could trade up from this shabby studio apartment on 13th Street, with its listing avocado green range and mismatched harvest gold refrigerator. But he stays because everything he needs is within easy reach. He cooks in his underwear because the kitchen and bedroom are one and the same.

"Why would anyone want more rooms than they can reasonably occupy?" he asks Carlos as he lightly beats three eggs for the pie's filling.

Colin ignores his mother's sideways sneer as he pours a second whiskey. He believes he came by his taste for the drink naturally.

"I'm Irish, for Christ's sake."

He takes his poison from a cut crystal old-fashioned glass. He adds a solitary ice cube. As he often does, Colin holds the drink up to the back parlor window overlooking the rose garden; he appreciates the way the yard light plays through the amber liquid and refracts in the glass' angles. The flowers and thorns glow golden through the spirits. Colin dangles the glass between two calloused fingers aligned so as not to block a single beam of light. He sniffs the drink's caustic vapors and then slugs it back in one gulp. He pours another.

MariaElena dumps the cleaned beans into the cast iron pot and covers them with water. She adds salt and pepper, onions, celery, salt pork, garlic, and a bay leaf. She reaches around her mother-in-law to pull the ingredients from their storage.

"Good thing Jesús is making his pie at his place," she says. "It's crowded here." She says this even though she misses her son's warmth in this drafty old house. Until he moved out two years ago, they hadn't been apart since she'd birthed the howling little U.S. citizen at Brigham Women's Hospital.

For the first year of Jesús' life, between maid gigs and breastfeeding, MariaElena halfheartedly studied for the naturalization exam. She failed. Twice. After that she set her sights on the passive Irishman she met on a Metrorail platform one lip-chapping winter day. She and Colin were married late the following summer – over his mother's objections.

MariaElena turns the flame under the bean pot to high and stirs it. The hard beans rattle like river gravel across the pan's metal bottom.

MariaElena's mother, *Abeula* Jimenez, died when Jesús was ten. MariaElena and Jesús returned to *el Estado Chihuahua y la Cuidad*

Asencion en Mexico to pack up *Abeula's* belongings. In the far back closet of the low-slung white adobe house they found two boxes of carefully wrapped *Nahua* iconography and texts, including rare *primitivo* sacrifice and cannibalism implements. Back in Maryland, as they unpacked the evidence of Jesús' other grandmother, Colin insisted that MariaElena send the iconography – anonymously and with no return address – to the National Museum of Mexican Art in Chicago.

"I'm telling you both; don't mention this to my mother – ever. This would be the last straw."

MariaElena curses in Spanish as the bean pot boils over with a loud hiss. Her fingers tingle crimson as she turns down the flame, but their warmth is not the result of the cooking heat. Like a volcano, malcontent simmers below her surface and at times her hands pang with longing. She has always known that one day she will erupt, and she is alternately fearful and welcoming of this prospect. Sometimes it takes all the grit she can muster to keep her hands from exploding into a million bits of shrapnel.

Old Mrs. Callaghan minces Chesapeake Bay oysters and adds them to the stuffing mixture. Her Irish in-laws had been disgusted when she'd made this dish for them during an American visit years ago; in Irish culinary norms, oyster stuffing was a slap across the shamrocks. But then, there had always been the impulse to slap between these in-laws.

Colin's father keeled over from a heart attack that had paddled toward him from the deep end of a whiskey pool for years. Upon hearing the news, his Irish sister demanded that the body be returned to Dublin. She wanted a proper burial in the family plot. The ensuing battle between the Irish and the American women became so heated that in a fit to resolve it, Old Mrs. Callaghan had her husband's remains cremated. She sent half the ashes to her sister-in-law, secured in a yellow and black Carhartt steel-toed boot box.

Colin watches MariaElena stir the beans. She is still lithe and nimble, he notes, still attractive at her age.

She was the first person he ever loved, including his mother.

"Who could love a mother like that?" he's asked Father O'Brien in the confession booth at St. Augustine. Father O'Brien advised patience.

Colin fell in love with MariaElena because she was lost when they met. Feeling disoriented himself, he'd appreciated the metaphor.

"Which way to Shady Grove," she'd asked?

Straight through my heart, was his first thought.

That was long ago. That train has left the station, and now they are two strangers standing on this platform. Waiting.

Jesús is the only person Colin still loves. He doesn't even care that he's turned up gay. He is in fact in many ways envious of Jesús' charmed life.

Colin regrets that he never went to college; instead, he followed his dead father's trail to become a Metrorail track repairman. He is envious of Jesús and his air-conditioned office job. He is envious of the Brooks Brothers wingtips that Jesús wears. Colin wears Carhartt steel toes over his wide, flat feet, just like his father did. He wishes they were steel heart guards; he is fully aware that in this house, hearts are in considerably more danger than toes.

Colin leaves the women in the kitchen and wanders back to the window overlooking the roses. The half of the dead Mr. Callaghan's ashes that were not returned to Dublin are sealed in that elaborate concrete urn jutting above the small goldfish pond. It has always been Colin's duty to feed the goldfish and tend the roses; to cultivate the soil in spring, to trim the spent flowers and straggling stems, to rinse the foliage with tepid water and Ivory dish soap at first appearance of aphids or black spot or leaf rust.

When he came in from an afternoon with the roses and his father, Old Mrs. Callaghan soaked Colin's blistered hands in more tepid water and Ivory dish soap. This softened the thorns he had collected, and then she plucked them with golden tweezers.

The one thing MariaElena loves about this house is that pond in the back yard. She sits among the roses in the humid summer afternoons and pretends to read. Instead, she watches the fish endlessly circle their tiny world, always moving but never going anywhere. From her seat on the short prickly grass she sometimes sees her husband at the window watching through his glass of yellow whiskey. He's like the fish, she thinks, circling his enclosure.

"Oh, *¡Dios mío!* but it's my cage, too," she whispers to herself.

On the day after his mother is buried, Colin plans to send the urn of ashes to Dublin and turn under the roses. He'll install a shallow pool and he'll circle it on a pale yellow floater. He'll drink to his father, whole again in Ireland.

Jesús lines the pie plate with the crumbling pastry that won't hold together. Before adding the nuts, he repairs as best he can the jagged rips across the crust's bottom. Then he crimps the edges exactly as illustrated by Betty Crocker. It looks professional, almost as good as his grandmother's. When he pours the custard mixture over the nuts a large dollop splashes onto his bare foot.

Jesús says his flat, brown feet are embarrassing. When young, his mother tickled them with her fingernails, called them *patas* (paws, like dogs). He covets his Grandma Callaghan's pink feet, still strong at her age. Those feet were made for marching, for standing firm.

Jesús confessed to Old Mrs. Callaghan in Wal-Mart two years ago. She was wandering aisle to aisle, searching for Ivory dish soap, when she found him holding up two different doll's dresses, comparing fabrics.

"Jesús , what are you doing?"

"Grandma, I'm gay."

Old Mrs. Callaghan looked away. "Where's the soap?"

She says she follows her church's teaching: hate the sin, love the sinner. But in practice she denies both.

Jesús places the assembled pie on the oven rack and sets the timer. "Viola!" he says to Carlos with an exaggerated gesture.

At 25, Jesús continues to sleep with, and talk to, this crusty teddy bear named Carlos that his father sent so many years ago. He also has hidden in a box under his bed an assortment of doll's dresses and hats that Carlos wears, depending on Jesús' mood. This includes a full leather dominatrix outfit. Jesús hasn't told anyone about the bear's clothing, especially since Carlos occasionally wears the child's burial dress secretly pilfered from *Abeula* Jimenez's hidden iconography. Jesús believes when the bear wears it, *Abeula* watches him – with glee – from her *Nahua* afterlife.

"Bedtime," Old Mrs. Callaghan decrees as she blankets the readied turkey with aluminum foil. MariaElena scrubs the last of the scorched beans from the stove top.

"Bedtime," Old Mrs. Callaghan repeats.

Colin and MariaElena were married 23 years ago at the Crofton Justice of the Peace's office. He was 26, and still a virgin. A two-year old Jesús was the best man. Old Mrs. Callaghan was not in attendance.

"I do."

"Yes, I do, too."

After the wedding, in the purple light of the hazy summer dusk, Colin brought the new Mrs. Callaghan and Jesús to the rose garden and introduced them to his father. Beneath the pink scent of American

Beauties, the boy lay on his stomach and twiddled his fingers in the pond. When the hungry goldfish suckled them, he giggled. Colin thought it the most beautiful sound he'd ever heard.

Old Mrs. Callaghan watched them from the back porch, her bony fingers flying along the rosary beads in a manic rhythm. She crossed her arms and looked skyward.

"Bedtime," she'd announced that night, too.

They all went to their separate rooms.

Two days after her son's wedding, Old Mrs. Callaghan kidnapped Jesús. She smuggled the toddler to St. Augustine for a proper Catholic baptism, dressed him in the same white lace christening dress that Colin had worn for his baptism.

When Father O'Brien dribbled the holy water over Jesús' forehead, drops pooled in his eyes. He cried and squirmed.

Old Mrs. Callaghan held him still with sturdy hands. "You're in for a surprise if you think this is the worst things will get, James – now hush."

Thanksgiving morning. Early, no sign of sunrise yet. Old Mrs. Callaghan struggles in her feather bed, confused, suffering with visions. This dream feels real to her, and not. In it, she hobbles for miles over a rough, tree-studded landscape, but she knows not where she is going. She knows only that she has to pee, and the only restroom she finds, which she stumbles upon over and over again, as though she is circling within her dream, is a men's room. It is buried underground and guarded over by scantily-clad men performing acrobatic tricks among the trees. Although none admit it, she knows they are homos.

"Come," they sing in tinsel voices. Their minted breath cools her flushed face. "We're your homo angels."

She barricades herself in a stall and when she ascends from the underground bathroom bunker a storm has boiled up; a thick cloud climbs the hillside toward her and the acrobats. It is like a black widow crawling up a child's chiffon dress – wisped appendages reach from the vaporous body, pull at the trees and hills and hoist the menace ever closer. They huddle and just as the spider-cloud envelopes them, she awakes.

Unfortunately, she has peed her bed.

Down the hall, MariaElena dresses for Thanksgiving Day. As a last touch, she hangs a tiny, brightly-colored folk art hummingbird pendant against her breastbone. This was a gift mailed stateside from her mother to honor the birth of Jesús. *Doña* Jimenez told MariaElena that she was like a hummingbird: beautiful, restless, necessary.

The first time she heard this, Old Mrs. Callaghan laughed.

"You're more like a mockingbird," she said to MariaElena. "You're always squawking, always imitating something you're not."

MariaElena swore back under her breath – in Spanish. She had refused to teach Jesús the language – she didn't want him to seem an outsider in his culture. She, however, easily resorts to it, especially when angry with her mother-in-law. Like then.

"I know you're saying something mean," Mrs. Callaghan accused from her lime green recliner. Her ankles were elevated, bound in flesh-tone compression stockings. MariaElena thought she was like an old coyote: nearsighted and lame but still able to hear a twig break across the forest.

"*Callarse, bruja!*" MariaElena whispered. She smiled sweetly through the sulfuric words.

Old Mrs. Callaghan changes her soiled bed linens and smuggles the wet sheets to the laundry room like a new bride embarrassed by the wedding night stains. She was flirting with spinsterhood herself, also still a virgin, on the rain-soaked spring day when she married the older Mr. Callaghan. On their wedding night, sodden from the celebratory drink, he didn't wash her softly with tender kisses. He shoved her to the bed and ran his workman's hands along her body. And then he had his way. His whiskey breath dribbled over her until finally he moaned and shuddered. The new Mrs. Callaghan refused to cry – this was her wifely duty – but every time he came to her afterwards, all she remembered was that night and his smell.

After Colin was born, he stopped coming to her.

Mid-afternoon now. A brilliant autumn sun filters red through the changing leaves of the maple tree in the front yard. For their Thanksgiving dinner, Colin removes the extension slat from the family's antique oak dining table. There are only the four of them, after all. Old Mrs. Callaghan palms an Irish lace tablecloth smooth and places four settings of her best Waterford china. Colin adds three cut crystal wine glasses and one old-fashioned glass. MariaElena contributes an oversized centerpiece of colorful handmade Mexican paper flowers.

"Let's do this," Colin says. He fills his glass with whiskey.

They dine family style. There is Old Mrs. Callaghan's roast turkey with oyster stuffing, MariaElena's black beans and rice, new potatoes (Mrs. Callaghan, in a begrudged nod to the Irish), cornbread (MariaElena), and Brussels sprouts (no one claims these). There is also a fresh salad with sliced avocados, and spotlighted in the wings is Jesús' pecan pie, beautiful with perfectly crimped golden pastry encircling a crunchy top of sugared pecans.

After the meal, Old Mrs. Callaghan ceremoniously slices the centerfold pie with a serrated silver knife while Jesús stands ready with the matching pie server. But the sugared pecan crust sinks into a molten center. The pie, through no obvious fault of Jesús' but obviously through some neglect or ignorance or mishandling, has not solidified. An unforgiving silence settles over the room.

"It's OK, son," Colin eventually says, "we're OK without dessert, anyway". He rises and plods to the liquor cabinet, his stocking feet thunk-thunk-thunking on the wide planks of the yellow pine floor.

He pours a short glass of whiskey which he carries to the back parlor window. In his mind he redraws the dimensions of the floating pool.

MariaElena watches him, and then glances at her son, who in this moment of despair looks exactly like his father did when MariaElena announced he hadn't enough *dinero* to buy her hand in marriage. She looks to her mother-in-law who has one crooked finger stuck in the liquid pie filling but stares vacantly at the faded plaster ceiling. The familiar crimson burning settles in MariaElena's fingers, and her left hand caresses the carving knife Colin used to hack off the turkey's legs and reduce its breasts to slices. Her gold wedding band clinks against the forged stainless blade.

"You know, James, my first pie didn't work, either," Mrs. Callaghan announces, looking from face to face.

She speaks quietly, almost a whisper, and her unusual tone is as warm as fresh baked Tollhouse cookies. In her mind she has seen nearly-naked acrobats cavorting on the low horizontal branches of a lost forest; she has sought refuge from the cold downdraft of an impending thunderstorm, seen a hillside eaten alive by a living cloud. She has awakened in a humiliating puddle of lukewarm urine, only to discover that it has softened a lifetime's accumulation of thorns.

She licks her finger. "It's soup. It's lovely pecan soup. MariaElena, get some bowls – and not those tacky ones from your mother's house. Colin, get the whipped cream. Hurry now."

MariaElena lays down the carving knife, and Colin abandons his glass of whiskey. They both follow the orders as barked. Old Mrs. Callaghan's crepe-skinned hand reaches across the lace tablecloth and finds the hand of Jesús under the gaudy paper flowers. Her bony pink fingers encircle, embrace, his short brown ones.

"Cooking is from the heart, Jesús," Old Mrs. Callaghan continues. It is the first time she has not called him James in years. "It's science mixed with love flowing from your heart through your hands to the food. I learned from my mother, but," she shoots a mean eye toward MariaElena, "I wouldn't expect that in your case. Come by tomorrow, we'll work on making pies. But right now, let's have soup."

John C. Mannone

Sing to the Fish

To the Damsels—*Clown* & *Black-n-Whitey*
and to *Bluey*, he was a tang. They never
felt the sting of your anemone
smile. I wonder if they could make out
the melody — the sound of your voice
thumping the glass aquarium. Must've
squeezed the air under their skin.

Bluey's countenance blushed, his caudal
tingling with thrums of your voice. Could you
hear his throbs, even sobs though bubbles?

Your daily song
cheered them out of prison, their glass
hearts. Big glassy eyes stared back.
Flit of tails buoyed their colors for you.

The blue tang, he couldn't stand it anymore,
flashed his yellow dorsal, jumped clear out
searching for you. Sprawled on your carpet,
he must have thought you'd rescue him.

He was still blue after his last breath
of sea as he poured himself out for you.

The Rites of Autumn

you've been building a nest in your head: from the twigs and branches:
the undergrowth of your body: you say all the ritual words:
forgivenesses and prayers: but like they were leaving your mouth for
the first time: born into the chilling air: there is no restraint of feelings:
you pull back the vines of your chest: and reveal the den within: sighing
with the open space: each year you light this necessary fire: begin the
burning and regrowth: the splitting open of seeds: the rooting, the
rooting: into the earth: now the bird of your spirit returns: refreshed
and ready for the new year

for Red Hand

Sleep with Accordions and Divers

it's all oxygen hoses and rusted diving helmets in your sleep: you're
curled up on the dock again: on a mattress of old maps of the sea floor:
old hose attachments for vacuuming sand: away from relics: while
dueling divers play *Sweet Gypsy Rose*: by accordion light: the glass of your
helmet fogs: you can barely make out the other divers around: but you
can hear a child giggling in her own suit: fuel drums uneasily next to
the winch: everyone is waiting for the song to end: all the gear is
packed: you readjust your pillow of sand: like heavy equipment hitting
the sea floor

for Lee Ann Brown

Stephanie Dickinson

The Muse Is A Blue Tetra

It was the summer of the oil spilling into the Gulf of Mexico. You'd been warned that the sun could blaze like a smoldering mango in your writing, and then go cold in an instant on the e-readers of editors. The bottom could drop after a few feet and go a mile down. Like most writers you waded to the edge of the danger zone, casting into the blackness. It was the summer of the final corrections on your novel that you'd been working on for years. Always there was more to be done in achieving the right balance. Responding to an agent's editorial suggestions. Wrangling, rewriting, reimagining. More criticisms. In the last six months completion consumed you. The revisions centered exclusively on the opening forty pages. For the first time the finish line seemed in sight. "We feel like it's close to what it needs to be," the agent's assistant said. The muse had brought you this far.

The muse is a blue tetra. A devil damselfish, circling the image and idea, and then struggling in the water turned cloudy. How do you see up? Sentences rush each other. There are galaxies down here and the muse fish carry tiny flames inside like distant stars.

Your novel had a long, tortured history. You began work on a manuscript set in New Orleans in 2003, having lived and gone to school in the city of ghosts who walk at midday, breathed the mealy texture of its air, drank the poison apple of its tap water. You loved the city's twisting jasmine and wisteria, the moss trees and St. Charles Avenue's big houses where cotton kings once partied. For protagonists you chose a childless African-American man and his white girlfriend who rescue an abused, neglected baby.

The muse discovers what is far yet close at hand. Time and space fade. Who knew of hair algae? Turquoise strings of silky kelp. That fighting fish make circles of wild metallic green and red. That they literally explode.

Two months shy of a completed draft, a tropical storm named Katrina formed. Little did you know that the winds were on their way, the gusting that breaks houses and drowns them. Feathers from birds, skins from pigs, hides from horses, the taking was coming. Katrina hit New Orleans on. August 29th. The costliest natural disaster in American history: 1,865 human lives lost, catastrophic levee failures and a great city flooded. While each day brought new horrors, you finished your pre-storm New Orleans novel and mailed it off to the agent.

You hesitate to use the word *my* or *your* in referring to the agent. It presupposes ownership of some sort. This agent, a highly respected New York representative of fiction is an erudite man who peruses the literary journals and wrote you after reading a story of yours. If ever you completed a novel please send him the first fifty pages. He mentioned he wrote many such letters/emails to writers whose work he admired. One writer took years to respond with a novel that the agent sold. You told him you'd already published with a fine arts press your first novel *Half Girl,* which took years to complete and even more to publish in such a limited number. It was as if it never appeared at all. "Then send me your next. You haven't made much money on your writing," he said. "Let's change that." Those words were spoken one day in December. A year later you sent him your manuscript. He responded quickly. "No editor will buy anything pre-Katrina New Orleans. Is there any way you can set it in post-Katrina New Orleans? Much to admire here, but I'm afraid you've got work to do. M is especially off-putting." You felt he'd pointed to a crane in the lilies where the bank was yellow from fisherman piss. "There's your target." Not the crane but the white blossom on the lily. The target seemed to shift, always madly unattainable. Would the muse lead you to that white blossom on the lily? You set to work revising your novel. The baby would no longer be taken, but found, its mother floating in the floodwaters. Now Bluejay was white and Memory African-American, both adrift in a flatboat.

Blink your eyelids and the archerfish spits. The muse water is driven through gristle and marrow, through gill chambers it lunges up, stinging an insect off a leaf or the tangle of rooted water lilies.

*

In the midst of these years of endless revision, slow-cooked fiction became less in demand. The first decade of the 21st century became the memoir decade, a publishing phenomenon. In the new millennium everyone was his own publicist. Traits to succeed in the internet age—aggressive, insistent, tech-savvy, unending self-promotion. Hundreds of thousands of blogs springing up and words pouring from every corner of the earth. Editors hungering for non-fiction in their e-readers.

You thought of your limited edition *Half Girl,* a barely fictionalized account of being shot at age 18 in the neck and face with a 12-guage, and the forever physical and psychological consequences. You could not write the story as memoir. You needed the distance between the first person and your protagonist. First person memoirs of meth addiction, sex addiction, compulsive gambling, suicide, incest survival, rape survival, bi-polar and schizophrenia, Asperger's Syndrome troubled you, the list seemingly endless, as if the most painful trauma of your life was its most saleable. Many of the authors you heard interviewed called the process cathartic. You sat in your cubicle mindlessly typing while you listened to the authors on NPR. It took decades before you could touch your material. The paralyzed left arm. Your muse speaks in lyrical language and lyricism went against you in the age of plain speech, irony and little descriptive furniture. Your job and its time demands, your struggle for quiet, counted against you in the literary microwave age. Eugene B. Sledges' *With the Old Breed at Peleliu and Okinawa*, called one of the finest war memoirs written, was published in 1981, almost forty years after he enlisted in the Marines in 1942. It took Sledges that long to face his war.

Archer fish. Archer fish. Their eyes below water take aim at the tree hopper, you could blink and miss the capture and lick. What is it like to be taken alive into another being, becoming food.

Half Girl's launch coincided with the publisher's collapse from nervous exhaustion. He'd created a press with international presence almost single-handedly. He's since recovered and the press is back publishing stellar avant-garde work. Your book was the fluke. The unlucky one. Trying to be your own publicist you sent *Half Girl* to a hundred high schools in Iowa where the book's action begins, where you grew up. No interest in a homegrown, corn-fed writer, one of their own? Apparently not. You sent the book to a number of women's prisons in New York State, the telling of a cautionary tale. No readers came. You were determined that the next novel would be published by a commercial house. You hoped for readers.

*

You persevered, writing by night, and by day formatting financial statements. March arrived. Tax season, busy season in the accounting work place. You were down to the first forty pages, having ironed and prodded and agonized over the likeability of your characters, over intrusive flashbacks. Five days after the April 15th tax deadline explosive gas swept through the Deepwater Horizon's drilling rig and exploded. Eleven men were killed. Millions of gallons of crude oil spewing into the Gulf of Mexico. It was nesting season for many species. Sea turtles, those creatures that lived on this earth for 150 million years were burned along with oil off the surface of the water. Other of the heart-shaped swimmers washed up dead and bloodied in oil. Females, you learned, often did not reach sexual maturity until age 35, and mothers coming out of the water to lay their eggs found not sand or marsh, but black oil. You knew there was no writing on earth, for all its beauty and brilliance, that could be as prized and dear as these sea turtles. The Kemp-Ridley's ancient dynasty. Then COREXIT, the dispersant. Hercules aircraft sprayed the fields of water with toxic chemicals. There was the live feed video of the broken underwater pipe that kept bubbling a fume of black oil. It was the summer America learned about the great undersea fjords of oil that BP had bored into, like those in Saudi Arabia that only now after seventy years were running dry. There were rumors that methane gas released with the oil could explode, that BP had drilled into a massive pocket of gas. Hundreds of billions of cubic feet of gas could shoot to the surface. Death to every living thing in the Gulf of Mexico. You called it the upside down summer. The phrase "busted well" found its way into an announcer's mouth, and then onto the internet. That phrase endlessly repeated like it was something fresh and edgy. To you it linguistically suggested that language itself was busted.

In the midst of this the agent said, "I think Katrina is still dramatic." He said, "The novel is ready. You've worked for years on this and now we'll see how saleable it is." And lastly, "I think it's a marvelous novel. Now it's time for other people to read it."

*

It is unseemly to be your age, to have labored in the belly of commerce, to have typed financial statements and answered phones endlessly, to write gladly in your cubicle late into the night after the office has gone home, and not have a book deal. At least this is the opinion of your co-workers. They don't see that you work to support your writing. To them you're a failure. Or a fool. "We're waiting for your overnight success," a partner says, with more than a hint of sarcasm. You are sitting at the front desk answering the phone bank while the receptionist eats her lunch. "How long have you been working on the great American novel? Fifteen years?" You feel the red heat in your cheeks. "Six years for this one," you reply. "My novel is now making the rounds of publishing houses." That feat in itself seems worthy of a nod. You want to tell him of all the work days that must be gotten through before you're able to write, all the waste and exhaustion. You'd like to say an agent with considerable reputation is behind your book. "Oh," his blond eyebrows rise; he is the one who two years ago gifted you the moment's bestseller, whether or not you were interested, and called it required reading. He's rich, from old money. "Do you have something coming out?" Then you have to stammer, no, not yet, but the manuscript is circulating. "Well, I'll be looking for your review in *The New York Times*. Cheerio."

The muse is a trunkfish. It masks itself as a tortoise or a sea turtle. Six bony plates shaped into a box and nothing but fins and naked tail capable of moving. The muse's tiny mouth is armed with sharp teeth, ready to gulp coral. A shape changer.

Weekday nights you write, but Saturday night is best in the deserted office for quiet. Your muse is a solitary one. She doesn't appear in the presence of others. Aloneness is her one requirement. Then 36 flights up in the Manhattan sky, the descent or ascent begins—either you fall deeper into concentration or climb toward connection. Both require shedding the constricting circles of self, until the world mind is breeched. Other writers have muses that appear to them only in the presence of others. There are those who sit in the Olive Garden or at The Bean, hunched over their laptops. Their muse drinks coffee too. That is as it should be.

At home there are cats; there is Rob, the hum and slam of a walk-up in the East Village.

How did you get here? An Iowan, you came to New York following a string of cities, the latest being New Orleans. Arriving here with an MFA in creative writing, you interviewed for an editing job at Doubleday, now merged into one of the publishing mega-houses. You didn't get the position. You took the first job you were offered, a word processor at a family-owned accounting firm. After all, what did it matter since your real life was writing? You studied with the iconic William Packard, founder of the *New York Quarterly*, with Roberta Allen, one of the pioneers of flash fiction; and at the incomparable Jill Hoffman's glass table Tribecca workshop. Since then the family firm has merged many times and while scandals have brought down the big accounting houses such as Arthur Anderson, your firm continues to expand. The Rockefeller Foundation, Rolex, the Salvation Army, the Municipal Art Society are all clients. You are a short story collection, a poetry collection, and one novel richer, although no one has heard of them, much less read them. You and your significant other Rob publish a literary journal.

In its tenth year, the literary magazine has been called "a beautiful grotesquery, an avant-garde twisted carnival." Perhaps your muse finds beauty in the unbeautiful. You plow the monies earned at your typist job back into the magazine. Once on a subway you heard a stranger, a professor, speaking of his publications in the literary journals crow, "No one reads the damn things!"

*

Things have changed at the day job. Your bosses are younger than you. Those your age come with baggage, the good kind---home, car, children, and bucks. "Oh, you're the arty type," says the new hire Judith, a Harvard MBA, who'll do part-time financial consulting. She's looking at the paintings and sketches by the artist Michael Weston that brighten your cubicle. You are constantly surprised by the accountants admiring Weston's art, as it could not be darker or more in the school of American primitivism. You learn that Judith's husband is a judge, that she lives in Connecticut, her boys are hockey buffs. She's a twin and her mother still shops for her clothes because she has the time and enjoys it. Judith is a slender, warm, self-possessed woman. Her clothes are tasteful, elegant, and unlike your own. Your clothes are too young. But they are all you have and you make do. Your baggage couldn't be more different. Living on wages and a debit card, living with a poet who suffers from Asperger's Syndrome and besides free-lance editing does not bring in money. His visionary muse rejoices as his focus on poetry is absolute, it excludes almost everything else. It is tunnel vision.

Your father died when you were three and your English teacher mother always told you how your father had been a Merchant Marine during the war, how when the others went on shore leave, he stayed onboard the ship and wrote poetry in his log. To be a poet, to choose words over a night of carousing made the disappeared father, all the more admirable. After your father's death, your mother gathered up her three children—all under the age of 7—to the farm where she'd been raised. She taught junior high and commuted, and with my grandmother's help, was a working single mom when they were a novelty. The farm became the loved one, the muse. You wanted to write from the beginning and you crawled inside books as the corn grew. Yet you were wild to get away.

The muse is a mirrored carp, its pearled scales reflecting each a Benedictine monastery, a water lily, a will-o-the-wisp's flickering marsh fire. You wanted the exotic because the muse thrives on what you know and what you don't know.

*

Where does the starving artist staring into middle age and beyond dwell? The arty type, the writer who survives on a wage and a debit card has to live somewhere. How about Third Street between 1st and 2nd Avenues? The East Village situated between The Projects and Alphabet City to the east and Soho and New York University to the west. There's a frantic night life around here, the 2 by 4, the Hookah Bar, Phoebe's. The old immigrants cleared out to make room for the new. This is the neighborhood of deranged women with dirtied sidewalk skin camping between the garbage of Pak Punjab and eating take-out. Posses of partiers from NYU tattooed like meth freaks had intricately needled them, too wired to stop at an ankle, but going for head-to-toe graffiti. Delicate-faced girls with trellises of dragons for arms. It's all about the body as platform. These are the monied who pay for a Cliff Bar with a credit card. Movers and shakers, on their way up, a bright generation marked by ambition and savvy. Your own was a collection of transgressive partiers; some survived sex and drugs, some did not. You feel no nostalgia for the hedonistic cacophony of those times.

When you live long enough in this neighborhood you know you're not getting out. The violent and violated settle here. There is almost a criminality to not having money beyond your 30s. Late mornings the more severely damaged come out and you wonder where they spend their nights: the white beards with crucified eyes, the young man in a woman's veiled hat boxing with a tree. Homeless blanketed on stairwells, stoops. The color of the tenements is sidewalk gray, meat scraped from the bottom of a kettle. Here you live in a five-flight walk up with the poet Rob Cook and your cats Vallejo and Sally Joy, and from the lower kingdom, house spiders and roaches.

For all that is wrong with the building, it is home. There's the Russian, said to have been a doctor in Minsk, who appeared as a home heath aide to the Polish man in #12. Rumor says he dispatched the old man; whatever the truth, the Pole died and the good doctor and his beagle, Behm, occupy the apartment. The elderly brothers Herman and Asher, who've lived together in #11 all their long lives, fight like a miserable husband and wife. When you first heard their yelling matches you were shocked by the ferocity and hatred. "Go to hell. Go to hell, you whore." "Call the cops. Call the cops." "You piece of shit." Sometimes it is 2:00 a.m. when suddenly it breaks out.

The muse seeks peace and beauty. Look at the Scarlet Reef Hermit Crab with bright red legs and banded lapis lazuli legs.

Eight flights up to the fifth floor, your door, your floors and ceilings, your roof. And in a city of homeless everywhere, your own roof is a beautiful thing. Yes, this is where you live when you don't sell out and you don't sell at all, when all you can do is keep striving. You are here with your muse among the others. Dark angels too have brought them here. Next door, the Chinese live. Stan and his girlfriend and her two sisters and her father and the Irish setters MooMoo and FooFoo. The sisters and father had no place to go after a fire in their Chinatown apartment burned them out. Their mother died in the fire and one of the sisters lost part of her arm. And Frank next door with his bells and bicycle and fishing pole, he who eats the mercury-laden fish from the East River. Here in the winter the boiler breaks, usually on a Friday, stays unfixed until Monday, stifling in July and August, herds of cockroaches, and each time you hear of a building that's gone down, a building that's burned, you fear your building will be next.

There's a new sign on the tenant's bulletin board next to the house rules. If your dog defecates in the building you are responsible for cleaning it up. Do not leave your dog unattended to cry throughout the evening and day. The police will be called. Everything is scarred here, self-defiling, even the animals. And there's grit in the air, a glue smell, a patina of musty feathers. If you had to compare this capital of the world real estate to an odor it most perfectly matched you'd choose a hen house.

The blues painted by the Muse are sapphires and the oranges are underwater flames. The muse is a dragonet with eyes set almost touching on top of a flat head. He is gold and red-spotted with fins of dark green eyes. The female is an impoverished brown and white. To court her the little dragon raises his feelers and stiffens his pelvic fins into an azure fan. Then he pouts with his lower lip. Unlike the Muse the little dragon breeds only once.

Inside #16 is Rob who had Asperger's before such a diagnosis existed, who was made such fun of in high school that he spent years holding a hand before his face. Who could translate that incredible ongoing pain into a chatty, survivor memoir? "Can't he write anything but poetry?" your mother, an ex-English teacher, often demanded. "No one reads poetry anymore." You met him in Jill Hoffman's writing workshop, at the glass table with candles and cheese, bread and grapes, and hours of critique and heady discussion. Sixteen years younger, almost a generation separated you. He hid his face in long hair, but when he lifted his eyes you knew. He was rickety like you. An oddball. He is not unlovely, quite the opposite. His looks make you think Russia, the steppes, Cossack ponies. His blue eyes, long wavy hair, his body builder's physique from lifting weights at the gym attract glances. He's sunk into poverty from the middle class he was born into. His grandfather, Fred J. Cook, authored sixty books: *The FBI Nobody Knew, The Cuban Missile Crisis, The Crimes of Watergate, The Nightmare Decade: The Life and Times of Joe McCarthy;* he wrote for *The Nation;* a liberal, he was called communist. Rob inherited the writing gene, but far from nonfiction, far from journalism. He's never filled out a tax return and he is thirty-nine. "You've built a holocaust museum out of high school," a therapist told him. You too come from the middle class, but have slid down into the impoverished class. This is the Bohemian lifestyle lived too long in oligarchic America between the rock of the dollar and the hard place of celebrity culture. Rob has four poetry collections, and his "Song of America" was reprinted in *Best American Poetry 2009.* He covered his face with his hand for years to protect himself from heckling. He still thinks he is being made fun of. "Yuck," he is sure a girl said to him. "I whistle when I see someone ugly," another girl remarked to her friends, and then she began to whistle when he passed. You wonder if he's not hearing voices from the old days.

"You must give the people what they want," Rob's mother says to me. "People like detective novels."

*

And then your novel went out. You tried to tamp down the hope as you feared hope more than anything. Hope is dangerous. Your agent sent out fourteen queries.

> *Memory and Bluejay: A Novel of Katrina* follows two unforgettable characters--Memory, a young pregnant African-American woman with her sights set on college, and Bluejay, her white boyfriend with ties to a local crime boss--who find themselves trapped in New Orleans as Katrina makes landfall. They embark on an incredible journey of survival through a drowned world, where kitchen chairs float and snakes lift their heads from the black-green water. Along the way, they find an orphaned baby but lose their own, witness a murder, and contend with looters, feral dogs, and their own ravaged emotions. In the end, the catastrophic storm changes them forever. In the midst of calamity, they forge a family.

Six editors requested the full manuscript. Harpers, Little Brown, Random House were among those six. You stood in that moment of truth and saw how quickly those years of work could be rejected. Any reason would suffice not to fall in love with it. How elusive that marriage of a book with an editor. You knew that Hurricane Katrina seared images of a flooded New Orleans into the American consciousness, that the media outpouring that marked the five-year anniversary of the storm illustrated the depth of emotion. Katrina was entering the realm of myth by virtue of its human stories. Like the San Francisco Earthquake, the Galveston Hurricane, or the Great Chicago Fire, there will be many retellings of Katrina. You'd had the hope that *Memory and Bluejay* might be one of those that brought this epic event to life.

The first round ended. An auction to which no one raised a hand to bid. Once you'd seen a fisherman in Texas nail a catfish to the pier and peel its skin with pliers. These were the moments of a writer's life when the skin felt peeled from the body. You would see the email subject heading MEMORY AND BLUEJAY and your throat constricted and your pulse jumped. You knew now that heading would bring more rejection. "For your information," the message read or often "FYI" and then a copy of the rejecting editor's email. Most you could not read although your agent's assistant said she'd read many rejections and the editors liked your work. Just not enough. It was time to say goodbye to the novel and those characters who could not grow, who were not complicated enough. Goodbye to Bluejay and Memory and all that blue-green swimming backwards, all that waking and sleeping. Time to move onto something else, time to be tough. The summer of the gushing oil was a harsh one. You no longer believed if only you could hang on a little longer your work would find its audience. When the crude oil spurted from the fractured well-head you knew you were busted too, that your timing and your talent were not first rate. You have no children, but if you did—a girl-child particularly—could you wish this path on her?

> *There are methane castles in the depths as big as buses*
> *and on the floor of the Gulf of Mexico the brown gunk settles.*
> *Your book is drifting down page by page*
> *to lie with the fan coral.*
> *You'll keep following the muse for she is delight.*
> *A blue tetra.*

I Don't Know Any Love Poems To Give You

The shepherd couldn't read; he didn't need to. His life existed between the soft low hills and the
sheep he tended. He had a dog. He called her that - Dog - because that was what his father had
called his dog.

The shepherd wasn't the kind of man to get lonely. He was lucky, that way. From time to time he
spoke or sang to Dog. He had no particular secrets, so it wasn't secrets that he told Dog. Only
perhaps that he wanted fish for supper or that he liked the smell of rain on grass.

Of course the shepherd had been taught about G-d. He understood G-d the way he understood
that sheep are calmer when they can see each other - he knew it was true, but not why. The not
knowing didn't bother him. The soft hills, the rhythms of the sheep, Dog, they were enough of an
answer for him.

One morning he woke up, surprised - he felt the need to pray; he wanted to pray. He didn't know
any prayers, so he began to name all the things around him.

The sheep's favorite grasses - Feathered Greens, Prickling Stars. A calling bird - Red Tail. Dog.
The bracing clouds - Curl of Hair, Heap, Layer, Rain Bringer.

Here, he thought, take these words and turn them into something worthy.

WINTER, NORTHERN SCOTLAND

Farmers are killing themselves with shotguns, with rough cotton ropes,
with thin syringes of horse tranquilizer. The horses have all been sold.

In a bar I am drinking American corn.
Doubles. Triples. The cliffs stumble into the North Sea.

The rain turns to snow and the birds
stand out in black on the white fields.
I think the shadows of the dead farmers
have crossed the ocean with me.

I face east: my favorite view here
from the concrete pier on the edge of town
to where the waves break dark and cold.

the rope he used to tie my thin
white arms behind my back

lead me to small cold bedroom
push me down onto dirty sheets
his mother gave him, little
yellow
flowers

it's dark except for slants
of light seeping in from
living room

I'm on my stomach
choking on flying feathers

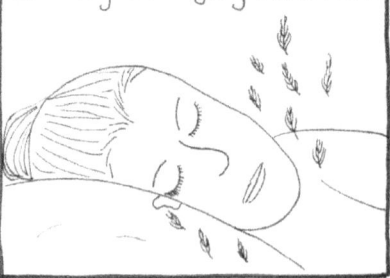

tears wetten pillow

Shiny Things

During the summer of his twenty-third year, Johnny Gorgeous started living on the beach in a rusted-out tilt-a-whirl south of Santa Cruz. He'd wandered from Seattle, losing money at the tracks, betting on all the wrong horses, until he was completely broke and stumbled on this place. The beach was mostly deserted and on days like these the ocean was gray and ashen; more dead fish washed to shore every day. Whole place smelled like old shoes and rotten ham. Sometimes, though, in the early morning hours, when the sky over the sea was pink and silvery, Johnny Gorgeous saw scavengers with metal detectors searching for shiny things in the sand.

He got up when the sun was too hot in the little red car he'd made his home in the tilt-a-whirl. He came out naked and stretched his legs and arms before he saw the girl with the old black camera taking pictures. She had frizzy dark hair.

"Hey," he said, "what are you doing?" He didn't think to cover himself up.

The girl took her hand off the shutter release and looked at him. She smiled and that sealed the deal for Johnny Gorgeous. Look at those big white teeth, he thought.

She said, "I'm taking pictures, what's it look like? How come you're naked?"

"Felt right," he said.

She took his picture.

"Say, you got a name or anything?" Johnny Gorgeous said. A nasty wave crashed to shore and sprayed them with water. It tasted like salt and ash and dead things.

The girl walked up to him and held out her hand. Johnny Gorgeous took it and they shook. She said, "I'm High."

He squinted his eyes. "Got any extra?"

She said, "No. That's my name. High." She laughed and let go of his hand. Johnny Gorgeous didn't want her to let go.

"Oh," he said. The bottoms of his feet were burning up, standing on the hot metal platform of the tilt-a-whirl, but he didn't want to make a big deal of it. Didn't want to say anything that sounded stupid. He said, "Hi, High."

Johnny Gorgeous gave her a smile, one of his crazy ones, where he showed his gums. Then he ran to the shore and waded into the water up to his knees. He bent down in the waves, letting the cool ocean rush over him. God, it felt good: the sand on his feet and the gray water and everything.

He spotted a tall and lanky figure walking down the beach carrying a metal detector. Even from this distance Johnny Gorgeous could see the goon had real long blond hair down to his waist. He knew it was the same goon he'd seen out here every day because of the hair and the sand-colored satchel hanging from the goon's shoulder. Johnny Gorgeous wondered if there was anything worth finding out here. He watched the goon for a little while, knowing the goon was probably watching him too.

When he came back from the ocean High was still taking pictures of the tilt-a-whirl. She snapped some close-ups of handrails and the little red cars and the rust covering everything; and then she walked to a spot in the sand far away or up the little path that led to the beach and she took pictures of the thing from a distance. Johnny Gorgeous watched her doing this, his naked body drying in the sun.

High walked down from the top of the path, her feet kicking up sand like she was still a little kid. Johnny Gorgeous thought she looked pretty happy just then. He said, "What kind of camera is that?"

High looked at the lens. "It says Nikon." She shrugged. "I don't know. I found it in a garbage can in an abandoned apartment complex where I squatted for a couple of months."

Johnny Gorgeous ran his hand along the rusted railing of the tilt-a-whirl until he was almost nose to nose with High. Then he stepped back because he was starting to get hard, sure he had the stupidest grin on his face. "Hey," he said, "let's go take some pictures of other things."

"Sure," High said.

Johnny Gorgeous went to go get his clothes on and, as he walked up the steps of the tilt-a-whirl, he was sure he felt High taking his picture.

*

They took a lot of pictures. Of rows and rows of sparkling dead fish; of a big green tarp that had washed to shore; of a sign that said "Danger: High Levels of Radiation" that High liked because it had her name on it; of a brown sandal abandoned on a big rock; of bottle caps in the sand; of the goon with the blond hair and satchel wading in the water, his metal detector sticking up like a shining tower on the beach; of the bleached white bones of a dead animal that High said was a dog and Johnny Gorgeous said was a hammerhead, even though he knew he was wrong and she was right, but he really just wanted to make her laugh. It worked.

They took pictures of each other too: here was Johnny Gorgeous kissing a real live crab; here was High showing off the snakebite scars on her ankle; Johnny Gorgeous sucking in his already starved-looking stomach, his flesh red and raw, his ribs poking out.

The picture he took of High standing with her arms outstretched in front of the setting sun and her whole body was dark as a shadow made Johnny Gorgeous sad. He thought about how, when the picture was developed, High was going to look like the lightest thing in the world, as if there was no weight to anything at all.

When they got back to the tilt-a-whirl that night they made love. It got cold on the beach at night despite and the whole thing started off as a way to keep warm, despite Johnny Gorgeous' feeble attempt at hanging the green tarp over the opening. He started kissing High. She didn't stop him. Her lips were chalky and chapped and her tongue tasted like hot, stale beer. Johnny Gorgeous loved it.

Then they were naked and shuffling around the little red car. It was pretty awkward because the place was small and crammed with his packs full of clothes and canned peaches and pears, and made for sitting, not sex.

After, Johnny Gorgeous sat beside High, sweating, the cold night forgotten. He said, "Know a place we can get these pictures done?"

High didn't say anything. The green tarp fell off, exposing a sky full of stars and moonlight.

Johnny Gorgeous shuffled through his pants pockets and found a cigarette he'd rolled awhile back. He'd been keeping it for something special and because his lighter was almost out of fluid. He lit the cigarette and took a long drag and handed it over to High. He kept the lighter on for a little bit so he could see her naked body: she had a light brown mole in orbit around her belly button. High barely smiled, taking the cigarette from him, and smoked it.

"How long you been taking pictures anyway?" Johnny Gorgeous said.

"Awhile now," said High. She was looking at the ceiling of the little red car. "Since I found the camera, I guess."

"You aren't one of those artists who got it in their heads this place is some kind of work of desecrated beauty? 'Look at the shit man has done to himself,' kind of thing? The post-apocalypse, it's the end of the world, and my eyes are wide, et cetera?"

"Who's that talking?"

Johnny Gorgeous kissed her mole. "My dad, probably." He kissed her mole again. "So. Are you?"

High took another drag from the cigarette and blew the smoke straight up. She said, slowly, deliberately, not even looking at him, which made Johnny Gorgeous kind of heartsick, "The fuck? I? Look? Like?"

Johnny Gorgeous' thumb was going numb from keeping the lighter lit, and the tip of his nail was really hot.

"What are you doing out here in this tilt-a-whirl anyway?" High said. She sounded mad. Handed the cigarette back to him.

Johnny Gorgeous thought about it. He said, "Waiting."

High laughed in short little bursts from deep in her stomach. Johnny Gorgeous liked making her laugh, even if she was mocking him. "Yeah," he said. "Waiting."

"For the world to get better?"

"Nope," he said. "To get into some cash. Biding my time, waiting for that lucky moment." Every time Johnny Gorgeous took a drag it made his lungs sting.

High took the cigarette from him. She said, "You won't get into anything living here."

Then the flame from the lighter went out. Johnny Gorgeous didn't say anything for a long time. He thought about the goon with his metal detector on the beach. Keep looking, Johnny Gorgeous thought.

"I'm hungry," said High in the darkness.

"I think I have some candy bars I got in a grocery store outside of Seattle in my pack."

"There's no film in the camera," said High, softly.

"What?" said Johnny Gorgeous. His hands were rifling through his pants pockets again, looking for the candy bars.

"You asked if I knew a place where we could get the film developed." He thought he heard a tiny sob escape her lips. "But there's no film in the camera. It's just fake."

"But it made the click-click noise."

"Shut up, man," said High. "I found the camera in a garbage—"

"Okay," Johnny Gorgeous said. "I get it."

Then he got up and went out of the little red car. The ocean breeze was loud in his ears and cold on his bare skin. He went down to the water, which wasn't far from the tilt-a-whirl. Out here at the edge of the world and at night, you could pretend there was no light anywhere, nothing shiny, nothing new. Johnny Gorgeous didn't want to think that, but he did. He went for a swim in the water, not sure if he could find his way back in the darkness, not sure he wanted to.

He swam for a little while, trying not to let the ash and salt taste in his mouth. Instead, he imagined the cold water was cleansing him.

When Johnny Gorgeous found the shore again, his teeth were chattering and his chest felt heavy, his arms and legs numb, his fingers stiff. High was calling his name from the tilt-a-whirl. "Hey," Johnny Gorgeous called back, "I like you, High."

He stubbed his big toe on the steps of the tilt-a-whirl and he cried out, hopping on the unwounded foot, trying not to fall off the rusted carnival ride. High hugged his shivering body. She took him inside and they fell asleep, her trying to keep him warm.

*

The next morning Johnny Gorgeous saw his big toe was broken. When he put his weight on it, the toe throbbed oddly like a toothache. "It hurts," he told High.

They were walking barefoot along the beach near the water, getting their feet wet. You had to watch out for dead fish and other things like silverware or shards of glass washing to shore.

"Looks like it," she said. High was being distant. She had this look in her eyes Johnny Gorgeous had seen several times: the kind of look that said I'm not sticking around much longer. Said: I'm already half-gone, don't try to bring me back.

"We should go into town," Johnny Gorgeous said. "See the ribs of Santa Cruz."

High was looking out over the sea. Johnny Gorgeous followed her gaze. There were big gray waves out there, blowing up against each other.

"We could take some pictures," he said.

"Threw the camera away when you went out last night to the ocean," High said. She was smiling, though. "What do you want cash for anyway?"

Johnny Gorgeous shrugged. Something washed up at his feet. It was shiny, glinting in the sunlight. He bent down and picked it out of the water. Bit down on it like he'd seen people do in old movies. It was a quarter. "Take a look," he said. Handed the coin over to High.

"Wonder how much of it is out here," she said.

Johnny Gorgeous was thinking about that goon with the real long blond hair down to his waist. Goon had been watching him, he was sure of it, just like he'd been watching the goon. First day Johnny Gorgeous got out here, goon was down the beach with his metal detector, searching in the sand. Goon had waved that first day, real friendly, like the world wasn't over and the whole ocean wasn't filled with dead fish. Johnny Gorgeous had waved back because it was what you did, but he never spoke to the goon. I'm just going to watch you, he'd thought that day. See what happens.

Johnny Gorgeous said to High, "Wish I had a metal detector. I bet there's shit tons of money out here. How many people used to live in California?"

"Who knows a thing like that? A lot."

"If I had money, I'd spend all day at the tracks in Del Mar, betting on the horses until I won big."

High stopped. She looked at him. "How stupid are you?"

"What?" said Johnny Gorgeous. "I'm lucky is what I'm saying. Always have been."

He shielded his eyes from the white hot sunlight with his hand, searching up and down the beach for the goon with the metal detector.

"Yeah," High said. "You're pretty lucky."

Johnny Gorgeous didn't know if she was being sarcastic and he didn't really care. If she was going to leave, she was going to leave. What was there to do about it but let it happen?

"There he is," he said, seeing the goon. He took off, running awkwardly, stupidly, because of his broken toe, kicking up sand and water.

The goon was a ways off, walking up another path, the metal detector close to the ground. Johnny Gorgeous remembered the satchel the goon carried and he thought about how many coins were in there. He thought about sitting in a nice cool place with money in his pocket, drinking a gin and tonic, living like a civilized man, betting on thoroughbreds at the tracks. If he won big enough, he could buy a horse to race; if he won big enough, he could repair the rusted tilt-a-whirl, start his own carnival, travel the state.

"Hey, you," he called to the goon. "Hey."

The goon stopped, turned in Johnny Gorgeous' direction. Johnny Gorgeous realized the goon was actually <u>waiting</u> for him. Like he had no idea what this half-starved, broken-toed boy was doing running at him. Made Johnny Gorgeous almost hysterical.

He slowed when the throbbing in his big toe became too intense. The sun was beating like a drum. Johnny Gorgeous was out of breath when he reached the long blond-haired goon, thinking he might faint from his racing heart.

Goon was as tall as he looked and had beady eyes. His hair hung down to his waist, thin as stalks of straw. The satchel slung over his shoulder looked pretty damn full.

They stood near the sharp grass where the beach ended—or began, depending on how you looked at it. "That metal detector work?" said Johnny Gorgeous.

"It does," said the goon, cautiously.

Johnny Gorgeous didn't like how the goon was looking at him, all squinty eyed like there was something wrong with the way Johnny Gorgeous was standing. "Hey, Skankpot Jones, what are you looking at me like that for?"

The goon just shook his head once, sadly, and turned to walk up the path back to town. Johnny Gorgeous grabbed the goon by the arm, hard, and the goon stumbled. He said, "The fuck?"

Johnny Gorgeous went for the satchel. He heard coins jingling in there. The goon was quicker though: he slammed the metal detector into Johnny Gorgeous' shins. Johnny Gorgeous fell on his knees in the sand. He said, "Shit!"

Goon must've thought that was enough because he turned to go again. Johnny Gorgeous reached out, his hands yanking the ends of the goon's long blond hair. Goon screamed and fell backward on top of Johnny Gorgeous.

"Give me that fucking metal detector, Skankpot," said Johnny Gorgeous. He yanked the satchel from the goon's shoulder, breaking the strap. Pushed the goon off his chest and upended the contents of the satchel. Shiny silver coins and dull brown coins and bottle caps and a bent-up, faded silver fork spilled from the satchel into the grass and sand. Johnny Gorgeous couldn't stop his eyes going wide at how much of it there was.

Then Skankpot got a good hit in. Johnny Gorgeous saw the fist coming at his face, thinking, how the hell'd Skankpot get up so fast, and then the sky sparkled white and yellow and green. He fell face-first into the sand.

He didn't remember much after that. He remembered trying to catch his breath, his face in the ground, his mouth open, sucking in thick spoonfuls of sand, his tongue coated with its hot, crunchy taste. He remembered Skankpot Jones saying, "My name's not Skankpot Jones."

Johnny Gorgeous rolled onto his back. He could only open his left eye—the right was swelling shut quickly. He saw High standing over him with the black camera at her face. She took his picture.

"I thought you got rid of that," he said, gritting his teeth. His shins really hurt and his eye was throbbing.

"Found it over there," she said. She pointed in the general direction of the tilt-a-whirl.

"Where'd Skankpot Jones go?"

High looked east. "Who knows."

"He take his metal detector?"

High didn't answer him.

Johnny Gorgeous tried to sit up. It was an effort to get to his knees. The coins that had spilled from the satchel glinted in the sun. He said, slowly, quietly, "Would you look at that."

"You got your ass kicked," said High.

"Look at the shit man has done to himself," Johnny Gorgeous said. He laughed and got real dizzy. Felt like throwing up. High snapped another picture of him.

"What do you want to do now?" she said when the silence had stretched for too long.

He looked up at High. He had no idea if she was being real with him. The sun was high above her, blocking out the expression on her face. No, he couldn't see High at all: she was a dark shape in the clear blue sky and blinding yellow sun.

"Head south," he said. "I hear Del Mar is nice."

"Chance to make it big," High said.

"Bet they have film for your camera in Del Mar."

High sat down beside him in the sand. She kissed him lightly on the cheek. "I don't know, Johnny," she said. "It's a long way."

Johnny Gorgeous picked up a hot, shiny nickel. "Guess we could see how far we make it."

In The Cemetery Where Jim Morrison Is Buried

At this bistro, I can't get lunch for another hour. Richard doesn't seem bothered, but when he can't get a beer for another twenty minutes we move two blocks away to a brasserie.

Here his friend Tom knows the owner and speaks in what sounds to me like fluent French, but he's an American. I eat fish, even though it's five in the morning in the States, and push my third café au lait away for a glass of wine before Richard and Tom finish it. The girl with the apartment key keeps putting us off. Tom explains he's taking triple his medication, a suggestion from his doctor. No one can get a word in.

Caesar is sitting on my shoulder, he says to me. Right fucking here, and he gestures to his left shoulder. He says I'm just like him, and it's just like when Rome fell.

I do not know how to reply to this.

Only without all the bloodshed, and he throws his head back and laughs. He has a dirty quality to his voice that I like.

We have to go outside to smoke cigarettes because even Paris must change. He tells me he was part of a religious cult. He followed a Christian Jew all the way to Paris. I believe I've heard this before on the news or in a college course. I want to go to him, to touch his arm, to hear him whisper religious nothings in my ear.

No one is forgiven, he says, his face close to mine. No one. There is no fucking forgiveness.

What can I do? I agree.

Richard foams at the mouth when he sleeps. I've looked it up and it sounds like the same throat problem that killed Atilla the Hun. Sometimes, I think he keeps Tom as relief—even with the nighttime episodes, Richard stands out.

Tom tells us over the phone that he will check himself into the hospital, but he shows up three days later and demands I make him some coffee. He gives Richard a cell phone he says is cheaper to use in France. Tom is sane enough not to want a big cell phone bill from Richard calling for directions all the time.

Tom and I smoke cigarettes out the window while Richard pulls himself together in the shower. I'm groggy and don't have the energy to pretend he's okay, or that Richard's okay, so I stub out the cigarette in our perfectly French flowerbox and play with my camera. Tom tries to make small talk, but I ignore him, making a big show of finding an adapter and charging the battery. By the time I'm finished, everyone's ready to go.

Tom has bought three cars in the past few months, which is part of his problem, but right now he weaves ahead of our rental on his new motorcycle. It's a BMW, and he wears cowboy boots. He's our guide out of Paris to the highway that will lead us to Bordeaux.

Richard has the shakes. I try not to watch his hands stutter across the steering wheel or flail towards the wiper control that he cannot shut off. Instead, I fix my eyes on Tom's bike, gliding between cars, leaning with his body into a turn. I notice this amazing feat—whenever he can feel Richard hesitate, he makes gentle gestures with his hand to direct him. I imagine him as a lover. I picture him as a boy with daisy yellow hair.

We pull into a gas station, Tom's turnaround and our takeoff point. He insists I buy him a cup of coffee. I'm going to call you tomorrow, I say, to make sure you've gone to the doctor. You do that, he said. Kick my ass. Oh, I will, I say, like his mother or his girlfriend.

In Bordeaux the streets are steep and cobblestoned. Richard and I crouch inside a monolithic church to witness the skulls of saints and ancient paintings hidden under soot. I tell him it's the most beautiful place I've ever seen.

The car is too much for Richard, and we fly back to Paris, cab it to the apartment, a huge extravagance by his standards. The cab, not the plane. It seems dangerous to rest, so the next day we travel by Metro to Pere Lachaise cemetery, the one where Jim Morrison is buried. I have insisted we do this one touristy thing.

Tell me, he says.

We are lost in towers of gray granite tombs, trying to follow a trail of spray-painted arrows, marked: To Jim.

Tell me, he says again.

Richard was once a marine, before I knew him, but I have seen pictures. He's not old, but now his face has a jowly quality I cannot accept.

Where would I begin, he says.

For a moment, I think he's asking for my help. I am relieved and scared shitless. I try to think of advice that doesn't sound canned. I try to think of what would work for me. I open my mouth.

He says, how can I get Tom to check himself in on his own?

It is then that I realize I forgot to call. That that day was days ago.

Later, outside this bar, Tom and his girlfriend are arguing next to one of his cars. She's crying, and it makes me happy, even though I like her, and I'm pretty sure she has plenty to cry about. Tom is wearing a black dress shirt and black tie under his biker jacket. He has a guitar case slung across his bike. I breathe him in.

His girlfriend is wearing a sundress. Her bare shoulders look raw. We don't acknowledge each other as we walk by. Richard and I give each other a look.

Tom walks inside a few minutes later, and a car horn blares without stopping. He smiles at me and tosses his hands in the air, as if to say, what can you do?

Not much, I think.

I have another Guinness because this is an Irish pub, and squash the urge to shout a request to the three guys playing on stage. I don't know how to say play The Weight by The Band in French. It's one of those nights that feel like a biblical song.

Richard stands up for the bathroom and bumps the table, slopping all our beers.

I wish my French were better, I yell across the table to Tom.

Tom smiles, I smile—we are both gleaming with defeat.

He says, I'll give you lessons. First, you'll read aloud a children's book. I have just the one.

I picture his tiny Parisian apartment, the touch of his finger to my lip, shaking his head and scolding my pronunciation. What is it they say about crazy? Doing the same and expecting different results, like the tigers at the zoo pacing a worn path through the grass.

The band stops playing. The place gets as quiet as a bar ever gets. Tom is still holding my gaze. I stand and bump the table, spilling our beers. In the worst French accent I can muster, I shout encore.

Dear Brigitte Nielsen

When Grandpa caught me watching *Red Sonja,*
all those Italian girls dressed in chain mail blouses

chopping at bad guys with rubber swords,
he was already drunk—it was Sunday, after all—

and since it takes almost nothing to enrage
a vet with untreated anxiety disorders, he went off

about how your place was in the kitchen,
not hacking down misunderstood monsters.

How women were made to care for men like him—
guys who marry women like my grandmother

who grew seven children in her private garden,
baby-sat me while my mother was on dialysis

and hardly ever interrupted her husband's tirades
after he threw a television through the window.

No wonder I dream so often of snapping
bullies over my knee like bloody twigs.

No wonder I fall for slash-and-dash heroines
armored against the charms of language.

Michael Meyerhofer

Psalm of the American Warehouse

I wrote *carpe diem* on a napkin
and stashed it in my wallet.
It was middle June, this warehouse job.
I had just turned twenty.
I had just seen *Dead Poets Society*.
I had just helped bury my mother.
And there is nothing
quite so lonesome as standing
between four-story shelves
under a roof of trusses and girders,
the untouchable skies of industry.
My uniform: whatever I didn't
mind snagging on corners,
getting stained with grease or blue dye
spat from the slushie machine.
My job: prowl those aisles
with serial numbers and a pallet jack,
searching not for the Grail
but the right box of gears, screws,
panels, slats of plastic and pulpwood,
haul the goods from here to there
and avoid those forklifts
steered by broken marriages
and thermoses full of Jim Beam.

I wore that note for twelve years
in the sleeve reserved for credit cards:
my protest against bundy clocks
and fluorescent tube bulbs
with their glow like bleached bone.
In other words, I forgot it was there,

went back to college, graduated
with a degree in sadsacking
then found it just today
while standing in line to buy laxatives.
The older I get, the more I think
we must each adapt a figurative stage.
I want mine to be Thermopylae
or an overstaffed emergency room—
probably, though, it's still that
warehouse where I dragged
my orange, makeshift wagon
like a kid in a steampunk candystore,
gathering whatever makes God-
knows-what with the help
of sawhorses and torque, schematics
like holy writ, raw materials wrenched
by better hands than mine into
some precocious, improbable design.

Returning the Lesson

Three days after my mother's heart
kicked up grave-sod like an errant mule,
my dad's alcoholic father came by,
carting along his oxygen tank,
its little red wheels squeaking down
a sidewalk of women in black dresses.
This man who drank straight gin
and didn't even know for years
how many children or rottweilers he had—
still decades before DHS—
sardined up in that country shack
I only saw once, as a yellow bulldozer
took ten years off my father's eyes.

They kept him away, so I grew up
picturing him as a rural Hitler
who dreamt of twisting out cigarettes
on the scrotum of the baby Jesus.
But there he was—that old grandfather
I'd never seen, frail as a psalm
with plastic tubing stuck up his nose.
This day will pass, he swore,
squeezing my hard shoulder. Meaning
of course my mother in her casket,
her hair all wrong, just a dash
between her first and last breath.

I nodded along, but wondered how
this sentence fragment of a man
ever managed to lock my father in closets
without food—my father,
who can do push-ups until sunrise,

who has three college degrees,
who could have broke him like kindling
but instead, took him inside
with one open fist on his shoulder.
I am tired of alchemizing the indivisible,
so here is the lesson I want to forget:
after every waste, the heart
like a dog betrays us but we,
when we must, call this forgiveness.

Rain or Shine

1.

1966

"Give me a minute." My father plants his elbow on the kitchen table, covers his mouth with his hand, shuts his eyes and furrows his brow. Smoke rises from the Camel in his ashtray as we wait for him to remember the name of a particular soprano. Then he pops his eyes open and slaps the table in triumph, like a kid resurfacing from the bottom of a lake, eager to show his buddies the shiny penny he discovered on its sandy floor. "Pons. Lily Pons."

As he continues to hold forth about opera, something in his eyes isn't right, like he's straining to stay on track. I want to shout, "Daddy, are you okay?" but I'm afraid to interrupt him. I remain caught between my fear that's something wrong and my irritation that he's pretending to be just fine.

By the time my mother tells me that afternoon that he's in bed with a bad headache and won't make it to synagogue that night to hear my speech, I've forgotten about his memory lapse and the strange look in his eyes. Not hear my speech? How bad could his headache be?

*

Every year, our Rabbi asks two or three college junior to speak at services on the Friday night after Thanksgiving. The topic—*"Is it*

possible to believe in God or to practice Judaism in an intellectual environment?" —
is the same as it was thirteen years ago, when my brother Joe gave his
speech, penned on stationary from my father's store.

I'd rather discuss the ideas of my American Literature professor, who,
while chain-smoking Galois, has pointed out in novels from *A Scarlet
Letter* to *Catch 22* the recurring themes of hypocrisy and repression in
society's institutions; but I'm no more likely to do that than perform a
strip tease. I deliver my speech from the podium emphatically, like an
actress in a long running play who has lost interest in her part but can't
afford to quit the production. I reassure the congregation that I haven't
lost my allegiance to my faith or to my people, that my Jewish
education, which has provided me with an identity and a connection to
God, is sustaining me at the University of Pennsylvania.

*

Nothing is sustaining me at the University of Pennsylvania,
where students are less interested in pondering eternal questions than
in possessing an abundance of madras shirts, Gucci purses and
Pappagallo shoes; where what matters is belonging to the "right"
fraternity or sorority; and where the most significant ritual is the
Saturday afternoon football game, during which students stand, try not
to spill cups of beer on their tweed suits, place their right hands above
their breasts, palms parallel to the floor, and extend their arms
horizontally to the right and back, singing "Hoorah, Pennsylvania" in
solemn unison.

I've saluted and I've sung, wishing all the while that I was
ninety miles north at Barnard, where girls don't care so much about
football games, fraternity parties or the brand names of their clothes;
where, on a rainy January morning in my senior of high school, a
student tour guide showed me around campus wearing pajamas under
her green rain poncho. Awed by the freedom she must have felt to
dress so casually, I wanted to change out of my navy blue jewel neck A-
line dress, low black pumps and tan trench coat into something from
her closet.

Although Barnard accepted me with a scholarship, Penn offered me $800 a year more. My father's men's clothing store had gone bankrupt two years earlier; he had started over as an insurance salesman, and although he had been named the top first year salesman in the country, he still didn't have the $800. Whether it was the difference in scholarship money or that my father couldn't abide me living in Spanish Harlem with a bunch of pinko beatniks, Penn it was.

I sulked for days. My father stayed remote. I took the train to Philadelphia to visit the school on Spring Weekend and watched drunken fraternity boys push a VW bug into the Schuylkill River for big laughs. When my father met me at the Providence Railroad Station on Sunday night in his grey overcoat and felt hat, he asked how I liked it. I told him it wasn't for me.

"What do you want? Buildings made of gold?"

I gazed miserably at the clapboard houses and pale green buds of maple trees floating by our car window during the ride home. I had done everything right—been a straight A student, head cheerleader, class vice-president, had a Jewish boy friend, even remained a virgin, never imagining that when it came time to decide which college to attend, a few hundred dollars would stand in my way. But there was no point in arguing with my father. He'd only respond, "You think you have such a bad daddy? Just wait until I kick the bucket. Then maybe you'll see I wasn't so bad after all."

The first time I saw BANKRUPTCY in bright red letters on white banners strung across the store windows which had for years displayed expensive suits, shirts and ties, I thought that whoever had put up those hideous signs must have made some sort of rotten deal with my father, taken advantage of his bad luck. That's what it was: bad luck, the same as if a tidal wave had washed over the store.

But by the time I graduated from high school, I had a different view. While driving home from Boston one night after he and my mother had been to the opera, my father blacked out at the wheel. The car swerved off the road and crashed into a tree. My mother, stretched out in the back seat because of a degenerating disc, rolled onto the floor and broke her collarbone. My father temporarily lost his driver's license and had me drive him to his insurance customers' houses after supper.

Sitting in his 1963 dark blue Dodge in unfamiliar neighborhoods, I'd finish my homework by the light of a street lamp and then grow increasingly impatient while he kibitzed with his customers like he had all the time in the world. When he'd finally return to the car and say with little of the salesman's charm in his voice, "Okay. We can go home now," as though I'd noticed a stain on his tailored suit, I felt ashamed for him, for his drop in position from merchant to salesman, for having fallen asleep at the wheel, crashing into a tree, injuring my mother, losing his license and depending on me to chauffeur him around. And I dared to think that maybe losing the store wasn't just a matter of bad luck. Maybe he had something to do with it as well.

*

My alienation at Penn soon soured into resentment at him. I became a chronic, silent critic of his foibles: his scrawled notes that accompanied my weekly $5.00 allowance; the mess he had made of my financial aid application—he had crossed things out, written over them again, as though offended by the invasion of privacy; even his need to cover up his struggle with Lily Pons' name that morning, and his failure to make it to synagogue to hear my speech.

2.

My mother walks toward me down the long hospital corridor, her pace measured, like she's trying to keep her balance with every step. She twists her mouth, and when she reaches me, holds me close. At 5'1", she's four inches shorter than I am. I feel like I'm holding her up. It's been a week since the afternoon my father went to bed with a bad headache.   His left side is paralyzed. I've flown from to Boston for the weekend. The doctors are running tests. Maybe he had a stroke, maybe a cerebral hemorrhage. To relieve the terrible pressure in his head, they've drilled holes in his skull.

I enter his room by myself. He's lying on his side, his head bandaged, his face unshaven, his eyes shut tight, like he's fighting pain.

I whisper, "Hi Daddy."

He opens his eyes and then closes them.   "Hi, sweetheart. How are you?" His voice is hoarse, as though I've found him napping on the studio couch in the den with the TV volume down low, not in a dim hospital room unable to move.

I tell him that I love him.   Then I walk into his bathroom, shut the door and bend over, undone, not only by the realization that he has fallen, as surely as our maple tree fell onto the roof of our house during a hurricane when I was eight, but by his attempt in his nearly cheerful greeting to protect me from the sight of him like this.

My mother and I eat lunch in the hospital cafeteria. We chew our food in silence.   It's February and my father is still in the hospital. Tests reveal that he has prostate cancer. The doctors don't know what that has to do with his paralysis, but as though welcoming an opportunity to do something, they operate.   I imagine what I will settle for: to have him live, no matter how frail or broken. "Mom, even if daddy can't get all better, I'm hoping that he can get better enough to go home."

She nods. Her eyes are always a little red now.

"Even if he has to be in a wheelchair—that would be okay."

She nods again.

*

In the third week of March, I sit with my mother, brothers, grandmother and my father's two sisters in the Intensive Care Unit. My father has contracted hepatitis from a blood transfusion. He's in a coma, his face and body swollen and jaundiced, his yellow eyes half closed and bulging, his face barely recognizable.

My Aunt Elaine suggests that she, her sister and mother all go out to dinner. They're hungry.

How can they leave, no matter how hungry they are?

My mother complains of chest pains. Joe, Billy and I take her to another part of the hospital for an electrocardiogram. She sits on an examining table in a small, cold room in her underwear, round blue pads, attached by wires to an electrocardiograph machine, adhered to her chest.

Someone knocks. A nurse opens the door and hands my mother the phone.

"Yes?" My mother asks and then breathes in sharply, like she's been hit. "I know you did...I know he was...no...thank you." She hangs up and drops her chin to her chest. "He's gone."

We encircle her; put our hands on her arm, her back. I stare at the top of her head, trying to accept the reality of what she just said.

For the sake of science, we agree to an autopsy. The doctors tell us that my father had cancer everywhere. He never had a chance.

3.

After thirty seven years of officiating at three generations' worth of weddings, bar and bat mitzvahs and funerals, our Rabbi has retired. A new Rabbi, younger and imported from out of town, calls us into his study to ask us what my father was like. We tell him that he had a great sense of humor; that everyone liked him; that he could talk to anyone, including the mayor; that he always said his three kids were his three million dollars. Things like that. Our conversation lasts twenty minutes, tops.

At the funeral, the Rabbi speaks in earnest tones about my father, as though he had known him for years. Annoyed by the emptiness of his obligatory praise, I get restless and look around. As he mentions how devoted a brother and son my father was, my Aunt Elaine, seated in the row behind me, rolls her eyes at her sister Marion. I turn my head around fast, wishing I hadn't seen that.

*

When we get home from the cemetery, the downstairs is full of people eating, talking and laughing. I go upstairs, enter my parents' bedroom, open the second drawer of my father's bureau, take out an oxford blue shirt folded around a rectangular piece of cardboard and place it against my cheek. Then I take the cardboard, grab a pen from my mother's bureau, crouch on the double bed and write him a letter. I tell him how dignified mother was at the funeral and how many friends are downstairs right now. I don't tell him that my mother put her head on my lap in the limousine while she cried because that would make him sad. I tell him that I'm imagining my favorite thing to do, which was to put my nose up against his neck, smell his Old Spice and make him laugh.

I cover the cardboard with the shirt, put it back in the drawer, walk down the hall to my brothers' old room, sit on a twin bed and read the sympathy cards piled on it. I hear footsteps. I figure someone has to use the bathroom at the end of the hall. I look up. Aunt Elaine is looking at me and the cards.

I feel caught. "He had a lot of friends."

"Everything but money."

Before I can respond, she disappears, leaving me breathless. Did she just tell me my father was a loser, that the people who sent these cards, who knew him all his life and say in them what a great guy he was are either lying or didn't really know him?

Looking for an antidote to her remark, I pick up the cards and reread what people said about Ike, whom his family called Izzy, short for Isaac, from the Hebrew Yitzhak, which means "laughter." But she has triggered my own doubt. Who was the friendly guy who loved to kid, close a sale, make chopped liver, go to the opera, who borrowed too much money, lost his father's business and died only a few years later? Was he an irresistible personality to whom everyone gravitated, or was he a screw up who "borrowed from Peter to pay Paul" until even that didn't work?

4.

For decades, I welcome anecdotes that might shed light on my father's life and character. My mother tells me that she broke off their engagement after she discovered that he had borrowed money from a friend, that she took him back only when my grandmother begged her to. ("He's sick, Bertha. He can't eat. He can't sleep. Please."). But although she worried again during their toughest times that she had married the wrong man, she remained a widow until her death at 95, because, as she put it, "No other man could hold a candle to him."

And my brother Billy tells me that one summer, when the store was sinking, he had barely climbed the steps of our front porch after working as a camp counselor for two months when my father asked him to hand over his paycheck; but e also tells me about the time he was working in my father's store in high school, and a sailor came in on leave to buy some clothes:

"Daddy sells him a whole outfit. While the sailor is trying on a pair of pants, he drops a roll of bills. Daddy picks up the roll, hands him some bills and pockets the rest. I think *holy shit*, but I don't say anything. The next day, the sailor comes back to brag about what a great time he had—the women he was with, how drunk he got. 'The only problem is,' the sailor says, 'I got rolled. Somebody took my money.' Daddy reaches into his pants pocket then. 'Not all of it,' he says and hands him the rest of the bills. "Daddy knew the sailor would lose his money," Billy says, his eyebrows raised for emphasis. "So he saved it for him."

Billy's reminiscences and my mother's suggest that in the end they both tipped the scales in my father's favor because they found it impossible not to love him (unlike my Aunt Elaine, who died two years after my father did, still enraged that he inherited the store and lost it eighteen years later). As for me, while I've thought plenty about his weaknesses and how they may have impacted my life, for solace, which is what I really want, I turn to moments like the following, which emerges each time like a shiny penny at the bottom of a lake:

It's a Saturday night in the fall of my senior year of high school. I come home from leading cheers at a rally on the steps of the public library for a victorious football game and ask my father if he'll watch Jerry Lewis with me on TV. He says okay even though he thinks Jerry is foolish.

I lean against him on the green plaid studio couch, still wearing my red and white uniform. He holds his Camel in his right hand and flicks its ashes into the standing amber glass ash tray next to him, laughing despite himself when Jerry sticks a cigarette up his nose or runs over to a cameraman and kisses him on the head.

Towards the end of the show, Jerry gets serious. He sings "Come Rain or Come Shine" from his album, "Jerry Lewis Just Sings."

The days may be cloudy or sunny...

We're in or we're out of the money."

My father asks me if I want to dance. I say sure. We stand up. I place my hand in his, he places his stubbly cheek next to mine and we do a gentle two-step in the center of the small room.

"But I'm with you always...

"Bertha, look at this," my father shouts towards my parents' bedroom, like he wants my mother to see that despite his loss of youth, money and the store, his daughter doesn't think her daddy's so bad after all.

"I'm with you ra-ain or shi-i-ine."

I separate my cheek from my father's to look at him. His eyes are closed. And he's laughing.

Oh

Oh,

The official state
organ ended this
session with
unwonted vigor—
a stimulus package,
a huge compromise,
a ratification.

fish

It was Tom's party. Kitty was very excited. She wore her favorite dress. We arrived by taxi. Tom's apartment was full of friends. There was food on the table that had been pushed up against the wall. I could not eat. The drink filled me up. I had another drink. Kitty started to dance with Macy. Tom said that Kitty looked good in her dress. After dancing Kitty tried to get me to eat some of the food on the table but I couldn't eat. I had another drink. Larry dragged me out into the garden. We smoked. I had known Larry a long time and Larry liked to drink. Larry was divorced. His wife and Kids were living somewhere in Indiana. Larry's wife wanted nothing to do with Larry. "I got hammered last night. Total black out," said Larry. I finished my drink. We went back inside. Kitty seeing Larry with me got angry but because we were at Tom's she let it slide. Larry got me a drink. Kitty said something about Macy that Macy wanted Kitty to go to her home and see something. I told Kitty to go. Kitty didn't say goodbye. Larry coughed violently. "Fish," said Larry.

I met Larry at Caomhánach's. The bar was empty. It was twelve. The kid behind the bar didn't look too interested. He was reading a book. Larry said we had to go outside to smoke. We went outside. Larry coughed violently. "Fish," said Larry. We went back inside. I ordered a drink. Larry told me a great joke. It was so funny the kid behind the bar laughed. Larry bought a drink.

Larry threatened to beat up the kid behind the bar.

I left Caomhánach's. It was dark.

I slept on the couch. I slept in my clothes. On the coffee table was Chinese. After talking with Kitty I phoned Tom.

Tom took me to the hospital to see Larry. Tom had a bottle in the car. We took quick swigs. I had left Larry uptown. He had gone to another bar and he got into a fight. After being thrown out of the bar Larry was hit by a car. The police couldn't make sense of Larry and so took him to the hospital. He had broken a leg. Before seeing Larry we had a cigarette.

Larry looked bad. I tried to make Larry feel good but the words I used were wasted. Larry was bad. A serious drinker should never visit the hospital or a doctor. Larry had found out that his liver was one drink away from failing. He told us that he was determined to give up drink. Tom gave me the look and we said goodbye.

We finished the bottle in the car and went to Caomhánach's. The kid behind the bar was very cold. We got our drinks and sat in a booth.

"Larry looked like death," said Tom. I nodded my head. I was worried about Larry. "We've got to help him," said Tom. "Yes," I said. We sat in silence. Other than sharing a few jokes at the expensive of the people we knew Tom and I had very little to talk about. Now and again Tom pointed to a girl at the bar and he always said the same thing, "I'd bang her." When he said "bang" I could have thrown up. No matter how hard I tried I could not get as drunk as I wanted to be and when I felt myself slipping I ran out of money. Tom said he would take me home. I was angry and sad. On the drive home Tom told me about his job. I cursed Tom I knew I should not curse Tom but I did I cursed him to hell. Kitty was in bed so I couldn't curse her. I watched television until I fell asleep.

Tom and Larry were sat opposite me. We were in a booth at Caomhánach's. Larry's leg was in a plaster cast. He looked better than he had in the hospital bed. The swelling was gone the discoloring had faded. Because Larry could not go outside the kid behind the bar said we didn't have to go outside to smoke. He told us to smoke "frugally." Tom went to the bar. When Larry struggled to the restroom Tom leaned over and said, "do you think it is right that we are buying Larry drinks?" I could have punch Tom. If Larry had been able to drive Tom wouldn't have been invited for a drink. Tom was one of those rare happy drunks. Something Larry and I despised. We drank to Larry's leg. We drank to Larry's liver. We drank to the kid behind the bar.

 "Wake up," said Larry. He was poking me with his crutch. "I blinked," I said and finished the drink. It wasn't my drink.

We removed the plaster cast. The kid behind the bar started screaming. He didn't find it funny. I used the ash tray and Larry used his crutch.

Tom   left.

"Here's to Tom," I said. "You shouldn't say things like that to Tom," said Larry. He didn't look good. I ordered two drinks. When I sat down Larry handed me a cigarette. The booth was enveloped in a cloud of plaster. I coughed violently and I saw them I saw the fish they were swimming they were small and translucent and they were frantic. I had to sit down. I blinked. I blinked again. They were still there out of reach animated swimming in the clouds of plaster and nicotine. "Fish?" said Larry. I nodded my head. "Here have a drink," said Larry.

Imitation Feast

The waitress walks into the banquet hall full of Hemingways. Every year she waits tables for the look-alike contest. No two Papas are the same: there are the tall, the short, the broad, the thin, the Times Cover 1967s, the Spanish berets, the Parisians. Eighty four pairs of drunken eyes and eighty four white or whitening beards follow her movement as she moves between tables, setting plates of marlin and greens and potatoes before them. All day they have been casting lures into children's pools, shooting lions with targets over their hearts with water pistols, running through the streets of Key West from cardboard cutouts of bulls, reciting lines from *The Old Man and the Sea* and *A Moveable Feast*. Lurking under the smell of marlin and greens is the musk of men after a hard day's work. They chew thoughtfully, savoring small bites of the marlin as they debate who the winner will be this year. As the waitress sashays from table to table, she becomes self-conscious under their gaze, slows the sway of her hips. The Hemingways grumble after her.

"This marlin is dry!" one Hemingway says.

"How hard can it be to cook a simple dish?" another says.

A third holds up a mojito, clinks the ice around and declares "Ninety-seven percent of the ice in this glass is below water." He slams back the drink and raises his gnarled forefinger for another.

When the winner is announced, a sixty three year old man from Tampa Bay whose crooked temper and six toed pet cat pushed him above the rest, the eighty three other Hemingways stand up and give three cheers for the man, too full of bravado and conviviality to admit disappointment or wounded pride. There are men in the crowd who have been there every year for more than a decade and not won once. All in the course of a man's life, these losses.

After the meal the waitress walks down to the shoreline. The winner in his maroon sash hooks his arm around her waist and they smile for the cameras. The other Papas engulf them and they make their way to the fishing boats. They line the rails and wave mock-forlornly to the shore as they chug out through the rough waves toward the Gulf Stream. Hemingways stand at the galley and drink mojitos and Hemingways stand at their rods and dream of green mahi mahi, silver tuna, blue wahoo. The waitress hugs her jacket around her shoulders and ducks her head against the mist. She watches the winner out there on the deck, fighting his line, his head turned upward in supplication. She thinks of her boyfriend, off in the woods with his friends, hunting deer, or in a motel with another waitress, his expression not unlike the straining fisherman's. Back on shore, the Mamas worry about what the Papas will catch this time.

Bait

What in the name of Sophia's marble boy on a dolphin was I thinking
the evening we opened each other up easy as a fork in a brick of tinned
fish, easy as picking out the dainty bones from salmon, the meat pink
as Phaedra's lips, as the inside of the cheek where a stranger's tongue
goes when he lays you down on the dock a hundred yards from the
party or on the carpet in a small room up your parents' hall, a man in a
hurry who opens his arms with a flourish, meets your mouth which is
dry as day-old sockeye, and kisses you rosy, kisses you until you're
pliant as a Coho filet?

And was I thinking that the day after, driving home through a
hangover fog the color of a tinplated can, my heart black as a dorsal
fin, the smell of bait on my thigh?

Accounts

so she says. she says I don't know
anything yet, I don't know
what to do now. she says.
so I says. I says you can't let it
get to you. I says. so she says.
she says waiting is the worst, worst,
worst, worst, worst. so I says.
I says take your mind off it, do
something to take your mind off it.
so she says. she says barbeque.

Yellow Line

threw a bicycle
chain. hit a gold-
finch. sounded like
church.
boiled a chicken
egg. snapped it
open. called it
container.
ran with it.
latched it shut
with paperclips.
broke it
some more.
taped it to a brick.
spotted a
nest. looked like
hair clippings.
hit the sun.
ran with it.

The Ninth Child

1) Names

Nine children lived in the house on the hill. Eight children had names: Billy, Maria, Tom, Sissy, Ian, Bridget, Monica, Carl. The Ninth Child was not called by a name. He had five fingers on his right hand and four on his left.

"He bit off his own finger," the children told the postman and the grocer and the priest. "He chewed it like gum. We saw the blood."

But children lie. The townspeople knew this and they didn't listen very closely. After all, it wasn't their problem. There was a woman who lived in the house. The children called her Mother, though a mother she was not. Mother owned this house full of rooms. The rooms were full of beds. In the nighttime she left the children in those beds, locked the door behind her and disappeared down the road. She was a younger woman, single and fat with a blonde braid that reached her waist. Mother had a number of bright colored dresses that stretched at the hips. She disliked all of these children, but it was the Ninth Child she disliked the most.

There was another woman who came around once a month. She was not young. Her hair was short and curled and a little purple, which was appropriate because her name was Mrs. Lavender. Mrs. Lavender didn't live in the house. She drove there in a new car, rapped on the door and asked to see the children.

"But," said Mother. "The children are in their rooms now. Mrs. Lavender, you always come at naptime." Mrs. Lavender checked her watch and smoothed her blouse. She looked around. It was neat enough, she decided. And it wasn't cold, though there certainly was a draft coming from somewhere. She could hear the sound of a clock. She had other homes to visit.

"Another time," she said.

"Yes," said Mother. "Another time." She shut the door behind Mrs. Lavender and watched the car drive down the hill.

Mother really didn't care for that woman Mrs. Lavender with her purple hair and her blouses and her files. After all, *she* didn't bring the checks. The checks, marked by the state, came every month in the mail.

It is true that children lie. But it was also true about the Ninth Child's finger. He bit off his left pointer finger when he was just barely three years old. That was four years ago, before he came to the house. The Ninth Child hadn't spoken since he'd swallowed his own finger.

The kids said: "Freak," loud, like they meant it, even though they didn't, not really. The Ninth Child knew this and said nothing back.

2) A Horse

There was an old wooden fence around the house on the hill. Past the fence, at the base of the hill, was a forest. Past the forest was pond full of tiny cattail islands. Swans lived on those islands. Fish lived in the water. From the house, if you listened closely, you could hear the sound of their silver leap.

The children weren't allowed to play by the pond, but they played there anyway, in the dark, when Mother's taillights had disappeared down the road. They leapt from their beds and put on their jackets and climbed through their windows. When you were small, they knew, it was easy enough to claim invisibility; to slip through a fence and then a forest, without being heard. At the pond they danced and ran and poured water on their hair. Of course sometimes they were caught. And when they were caught Mother smacked their ears with a newspaper and turned the locks on their doors.

But the Ninth Child didn't care. Because behind the pond, where the grass was tall and dry, he had discovered a horse.

"Hi," said the child to the horse and the horse shook his head of sleep.

"Hello?" said the Ninth Child again.

"Hi," said the horse. "Hi there." He put his nose onto the Ninth Child's shoulder, breathed out, then in.

"You are quite cold," said the horse.

"Yes," said the Ninth Child, and they stood like that, regarding one another, until the horse began to doze and the child headed upwards to the house on the hill.

Every night, the child went to the horse. The horse was named Blue, but his coat was black.

"Like ink," said child.

The horse said, "I'll tell you about ink. Don't let them give you a tattoo, because that means they own you." The horse knew, because he had a tattoo with seven blue numbers on the inside of his upper lip. The Ninth Child had seen it, had pressed his finger against the slick, rubbery skin.

"You taste like salt," the horse said.

"Yes," said the Ninth Child.

"And you smell like water." He pressed his face against the horse's shoulder.

"Right," said the horse.

The house on the hill had rules. For example, at 6 o' clock, the children gathered around a long table in the dining room for supper.

They prayed to Jesus and ate hot dogs and applesauce. Every evening the children had hotdogs and applesauce and a jar full of thin blue milk. The Ninth Child drank the milk and filled his jar full of applesauce. It was true he was getting skinnier in the shoulders and face, because he'd scooped all his applesauce into the jar and fed it to the horse. His t-shirts and sweaters hung around his body and the other kids said, "Look at his dress! Look, he's wearing a *dress!*" Mother approved. She said you could count the ribs of Christ like coins. The Ninth Child counted minutes. He counted each minute that passed until he could slip through the window and fence and go to the pond.

"I've been thinking," the child told the horse, "It might be time to get out of here."

"Me, too," said the horse. "In the winter the grass freezes and tastes like metal."

"In the winter," said the Ninth Child, "the pond is frozen and the fish don't leap."

The horse nodded. "Come for a ride," he said and bent his great bony knees so the child could climb on. The child pressed his heels against the horse's side and they rode towards the forest.

Time passed; ten minutes, an hour. It might have been more. The horse was strong, and the Ninth Child was warm and awake. But from the road, two headlights shone. Children appeared from behind the cattails and glided towards the house, hair and skin dark and wet. Swans stretched their necks and shifted their wings. The fish continued to jump.

"I should go back," said the Ninth Child, thinking about the dry smack of a newspaper on his ears. The horse didn't argue. The child slid to the ground. Behind them the birds were opening their eyes and shuffling their wings.

3) Birds

"Fly! Fly!" said the children in the house, the brown haired children, the blonde haired children, the children with hardly any hair at all. These were Nobody's Children. They landed in corners like birds. They preened and slinked and swooped with their hands. They dressed in sweaters and skirts and jeans and caps. They left things on the ground: markers, pop tops, drawings and notes; candy, bee bees, spitballs, pencils.

Each Sunday Mother stripped the children of their clothes and scrubbed. Mrs. Lavender, wearing lavender, was coming more often now. One by one the children came down and smiled at Mother and Mrs. Lavender. The children knew Mrs. Lavender knew about them, because she had folders of paper stacked neatly in a tote bag. She knew, for example, that none of them had mothers and all of them had teeth.

4) Winter

Winter came. The leaves had fallen from the trees and the branches scraped the windows dryly. The child no longer ate. He was so weak now that he could not walk down to see the horse. Every step made him gasp and wheeze, and the horse missed him and paced the perimeters of the pond.

In the house the child slept, or pretended to sleep, and dreamed about the horse, and the horse's blue number tattoo. He dreamed he had blue numbers instead of teeth. Dreams opened a big sharp tooth in his stomach. He knew when Mrs. Lavender came into the room. She was ancient, and whole, and the child tried to open his eyes.

"There are no legal guardians," Mrs. Lavender told the room.

What she didn't know was that the child belonged to the horse.

"They can't own me if they can't hear me," he'd told Blue.

"I know what you mean," said Blue and lowered his head.

5) The Nightmares

Once upon a time, the Ninth Child fought the Nightmares; went after them with his very own teeth. But the Nightmares were too fast and thin for blood. When he raised his hand to cover his scream, he caught his own finger instead. He bit through flesh and then through bone and when the child called out, he found his throat was full and sore and that he could no longer speak.

Now, the Nightmares were tangling the branches in the trees outside. Now, they were coming into the house. Mother had been taken away and The Ninth Child tried to keep his eyes open. Mrs. Lavender stood over him and said, "Easy, child. Sleep child, sleep," but across the hallway the Nightmares hissed. The Ninth Child felt the cold press his chest. It wasn't Mrs. Lavender who stood over him, but a doctor in a long, white coat.

"I'm afraid it's too late," said the doctor professionally. "A matter of time now, a matter of time." A stethoscope swung at his chest. The Ninth Child thought of clocks until the tocking stopped.

6) Stars

When The Ninth Child opened his eyes it was the middle of the night and the stars were pressing against his window like fingerprints. Downstairs it was quiet. The children slept but The Nightmares blinked through the holes in their doors. The Ninth Child was not afraid. He went to the window and opened it. He climbed onto the roof, shimmied down the drainpipe and ran barefoot to the pond. The horse shone in the dark and the stars and moon slid against his back like water. The Ninth Child caught them in his cupped hands and poured them down his throat. They were warm like soup, but dry like dust. He could breathe now. He breathed in, then out. In the house on the hill Mrs. Lavender shadowed the bed.

The Ninth Child took the horse's mane in his hand and climbed onto his back. The horse trotted quietly through the fields and the child rode. When the Nightmares started crawling down the side of the house, the Ninth Child leaned down and said, "to the water, Blue, just a little bit faster." And Blue turned to the pond. A thin layer of ice had formed but Blue broke it easily with his knees. Fish gathered at the surface. Birds landed on the backs of the child and the horse. When the water reached his chest Blue stopped to drink and eat the pond grass, which was so tall, it was as tall as the Ninth Child on top of the horse. The child rested his head on the horse's mane and closed his eyes. An ambulance screeched from the road but by then Blue was swimming, his legs churning, his tail floating. The birds flew behind and above. The Ninth Child reached out and let the water cool his palms and wrists.

7) Children

Eight children were woken by sirens. Eight children howled and shook and scattered like seeds through doorways and staircases. Their eyes flashed and blinked. Outside their windows they had seen the Nightmares crouch.

VIII) Mothers

"I had a mother, once," the child told the horse, as the water reached his neck.

"So did I," said the horse.

Serious People

I couldn't go in or out of our building without discovering my landlady Mrs. SendInTheIdiots maneuvering galvanized garbage cans from the basement to the curb. She seemed to be driven by the genetic imperative of animals traveling thousands of miles on a dangerous journey to mate, though she moved more like those sea tortoises who lay eggs on a Galapagos beach and die shortly thereafter. Once they were curbside, I had no idea at all who picked them up or where they were taken, these garbage cans of hers, it didn't seem to be the Sanitation Department, nor could I imagine why there might have been a limitless cache of galvanized containers—many of them brand new--in the subterranean depths of the building itself.

Most apartment buildings in midtown Manhattan are maintained by "supers," many have doormen. Ours had Mrs. SendInTheIdiots. I never learned my landlady's actual name, by the way, nor, as far as I know, was it ever learned by any of her tenants. (Rent checks were made out to H. H. BLOOMENTHAL and SONS, LLC, which managed the building, and I actually called them once, wanting to know, driven by a kind of careless curiosity. "Who wants to know?" came the reply, then the man on the other end, too Yiddish to be one of the sons and too young to be the old man, slammed down the phone.) Her postbox read simply LANDLORD S. Several times I heard her use her surname in conversation, but she said it so quickly that I heard her name only phonetically, seven syllables crammed into five or six, so it came out Mrs. SendInTheIdiots and she became that person to me for the rest of the time I lived there. Mrs. SendInTheIdiots. She was Eastern European, with an accent you could cut with a knife.

This was the autumn of 2002. The preceding spring I'd taken my Master of Fine Arts degree in Creative Writing from Columbia. A search for work was dulling some of the elation I'd felt at graduation.

An MFA was like joining the Army and being issued a bazooka with a range of ten feet, and the only target I'd hit so far was this apartment on the East side, 56th Street between First and Second, once a gentrified area of the city known as Sutton Place, which, if you defined its boundaries broadly enough, included the tiny, converted brownstone where I was living. Those first few months were largely divided between looking for a job while watching my funds deplete with alarming determination, and trying to get anything in my apartment to work. My landlady, the one who had a seven syllable name that for reasons best known to her she squeezed into six-or-under, was who I saw about the latter. Imagine getting blood from a stone. Each of my complaints and requests for assistance was either not her fault or not within her powers to remedy, beginning with the basics, essentials such as hot water, and ending with my request for new locks.

Mrs. SendInTheIdiots was a formidable presence. A look of fury could flash across her face fully capable of dropping a SCUD missle mid-flight. Fortunately, I was spared that. She liked me. She liked writers, and I don't think I would have gotten the apartment had I been schooled as anything else. From a painter who worked exclusively in oils, she learned that Van Gogh had enjoyed the goodwill of his landlady, a widow named Mrs. Venissac. This came up when I asked about a cheap print of Van Gogh's Yellow House on her kitchen wall. Apparently Van Gogh had been the widow Venissac's tenant in that very yellow house while living in France in the village of Arles. She'd rented Van Gogh several rooms on the ground floor initially, and when he couldn't any longer afford the space, she allowed him two rooms for nothing in the back of the yellow house in the painting, feeding him for free and lending him money when two rooms for free weren't enough to sustain him. The good widow Venissac was a woman who saw as *her* art the nurturing of artists, and Mrs. SendInTheIdiots modeled her life accordingly, I gathered.

As time went on, she began inviting me into her kitchen for afternoon tea, and it was during these teas that her hands came to light. Though she had known hard work, her fingers were delicate and girlish. She was vain about this. Not many widows her age could still remove their wedding rings without the benefit of soap, she assured me, and she would present this to me as a kind of parlor trick. This was several years ago and I may be misremembering. Maybe she didn't actually slip the ring from her finger and wave it beneath my nose, awaiting my reaction, daring me to take it for granted. Nonetheless I see myself sitting there in her kitchen the way I imagine actors must face one another when auditioning for a part, for that's how I felt. I felt like I was reading for a role, auditioning for a part. Why exactly was I there? I found myself trying to tease out my motivations as well as her own. What need, precisely, was she expecting me to meet? And what difference could it make to anyone how she took off a ring? And how much tea could the human bladder hold?

It was during one of these teas that she told me about the problems of our friend Rafael. Rafael was our neighborhood dry cleaner. He had come to America from Tehran where he played with the Iranian equivalent of its national orchestra. Now he was moonlighting in Broadway pit bands, woodwinds primarily. Broadway had all but shut down after the World Trade Center was leveled by terrorists the year before but now that the shows were up and running again, he'd been working fairly regularly. I looked for reasons to throw business his way in order to hear his stories about which TV star couldn't carry a tune in a bucket or which big-throated Broadway mama was also a whore and a lush. He was easily plied with ice cream. Rafael was an ice cream freak so I usually picked up a Dove Bar whenever there was dry cleaning. He liked Dove Bars.

Rafael had family back in Tehran as well as a wife and children here, and they were often on his mind. The attack on the World Trade Center had changed the climate of the city. There was some kind of sweep underway by the immigration services and while he'd recently won an appeal, he wasn't sure how long it would stand. Rafael 's eyes were hooded and focused and he always seemed to be looking over your shoulder to see who was coming through the door next.

II.

My day often began with a list. Mrs. SendInTheIdiots wrote on whatever happened to be handy, in this case a mini-box of Rice Crispies torn at the seams so that the inside of the front cover served as a writing surface. There were several things she wanted me to do for her, pick up some rock salt to keep the front stoop clear in the months ahead, hand-deliver a pair of small boxes, order some pvc, small errands I ran for her in return for being behind in my rent, most of these in Murray Hill on this particular morning. One entry on the list was puzzling: BISON ITCHES. She'd been in this country for years but had yet to master English, so I put it near the bottom of my to-do list, saying it aloud in varying intonations, which was something I had learned to do which any message she left me in writing, say it aloud and quickly and with different stresses on the syllables, and eventually this paid off. What she wanted was for me to stop at Sarge's, one of her favorite deli's in the city, and pick up her usual deli order: lox and a bagel with cream cheese for her lunch, tomato on the side, no pickle unless they were the big, hard ones, and for her dinner a roast beef sandwich on rye, cheddar, and coleslaw. It was simple once you got the hang of it, BUY SANDWICHES.

Because we had no super, everything had to be jobbed out to plumbers, house painters, plasterers, heating contractors, window glazers, electricians and a bevy of other craftsman. This was no small work. Ours was an old building and it was no small work to keep that building going. I've made fun of Mrs. SendInTheIdiots for being hard to deal with when I came with some small request for an improvement in my living conditions, but in effect she was the General Contractor for all of this. I'm sure she had her hands full. There were periods when the building seemed to be overrun with workmen. There were periods when the building was a symphony of hammering , drilling, pounding, table-sawing, shouts and crashes and booms.

She'd been busy earlier with broom and mop in the front hall and when I returned she was talking to the workmen who were loading bags of sand into the hold of their truck. No broom now, no mop. One was struggling with the bags from a high pile there at the rear of the building, then slinging it off to the second who stood behind the truck and was virtually catching these on the fly. They were syncopated to one another. As the first man tossed, the second man turned from the truck. Once he had it, he'd turn the other way and toss it into the hold. The first man was ready to go again by this point. It was hard work and they'd been plugging away at a fairly low beat. She invited me for tea. She told me Rafael hadn't won his appeal after all, the decision had been reversed, just as he'd feared, and he only had one more appeal to make before he and his family would be asked to leave the country.

We must have made quite a pair sitting there in her kitchen those many afternoons. Her hands, like vessels in the sunlight. My hopes of being a published writer disappearing in much that same light. I realize now that there is something sweet about two people at different stages of their lives waiting for something good to happen, and over tea that afternoon I told her—I hope *sweetly*--of bluffing my way into the offices of Esquire and demanding an interview with its fiction editor, leaving out the part about how I was stared down by a thick-set, cheerful security guard old enough to be my great-grandfather.

I went by to see Rafael the next day and he seemed to be in pretty good spirits, considering. I'd been out running morning errands. He had a lot of problems with roaches in his shop and he was working in a corner with what they call a "pocket pistol." He twirled it on his finger as he walked from nook and cranny to nook and cranny. He tucked it in the waist of his pants otherwise. It appeared to be minutely calibrated and he changed its settings several times as we talked. He'd get down on his knees and squeeze a long stream of spray into the hidden reaches of the wall and say something like, My Condolences, or, Hasta La Vista, Baby, both of these like Arnold Schwarzenegger. Hasta La Vista, Babby, Hassta La Vista, Babby. He was trying to learn the language by watching DVDs at night, and he was drawing out the words in a way that was mostly tongue, not throat. I Love You Babby, You're All I've GOT! POW!.

Rafael had this little heart-shaped face and he wore pink rubber boots when he was spraying for roaches, so there was probably no one who looked less dangerous than Rafael-the-dry-cleaner, but I still thought that wasn't funny. I knew he was under pressure, afraid for those he loved, and I felt sorry for Rafael, but like I said, the climate had changed and I didn't think that was appropriate.

Before the month was out he threw a going-away party for himself and I was invited. I only knew a few of the people there, Mrs. SendInTheIdiots to name one, Buddy to name another. Buddy was from Chengdu, about as far west as you can go in China without living in Tibet. He was a waiter in a szechuan restaurant in our neighborhood called Bobo's, where nothing was ever right. Buddy always brought the table one glass of water, even if you were a party of twenty people, apparently expecting the group to share it, and that water was always warm. Next he brought a bowl of complimentary warm noodles from the chef, always cold. The fortunes in the fortune cookies were in Mandarin. Once, out of curiosity, I went onto Google and did a translation. One of the fortunes read, *In China, as many ducks as people*. Another said China was the source of the last two pandemics. Not once was my bill correct. Never. Buddy again. And should I bring this to the poor fellow's attention his eyes would dart suddenly upward, as if looking for the chart of base-ten mathematics that he had taped to the ceiling.

There must have been twenty guests in all at Rafael's farewell, including half a dozen from Russia, all of them musicians of one sort or another. When I walked in, Buddy was playing something dirge-like on a French horn. It was something he'd written in honor of the small town where Rafael was born, which is in northwest Iran near the Russian border, I learned. A few others had brought bottles of vodka. They were talking about half-tones and telling stories about pranks they'd played, like soaping the pegs of some second violin's instrument so that it slipped out of tune during Bizet. I found myself a job in the kitchen, slicing the bread for dinner. While I was wiping down the cutting board I saw one of the Russians carefully lift a violin from an open case, the instrument in oilcloth. After peeling away its covering and tuning the instrument by its pegs, he looked to the right, then looked to the left, as if there might have been tombstones in either direction, then he put a little handkerchief beneath his chin and rested the violin on the handkerchief, and as he began to play and others answered on their instruments, I thought what a great afternoon I was having, how lucky I was to be there.

A refugee from the Ukraine named Misha had come to cook a dinner of pork and peppers and tomatoes. He'd brought his own cauldron. Seriously. A cast iron cauldron, something straight from MacBeth, and now that I had the bread sliced I was in charge. Misha brought his own herbs as well and said the herbs would help the grease to absorb and they seemed to be doing that. He said to keep stirring it on a slow fire and I was. Two of the other men in Rafael's tiny kitchen were from St. Petersburg, and they had the kind of bar-fight courage I think of when I think of St. Petersburg, because I've heard stories, but they weren't thugs or bullies, even when they were drinking vodka, and they were drinking vodka. Everyone was but me. Rafael came into the kitchen when the violinist was playing particularly well and tapped his ear, he wanted me to listen. I didn't understand at first what he meant, so he put his head next to mine and put his arm around my shoulder, and we listened together. He offered me his glass. I took a big drink and swallowed it, even though it was a kind of raw Russian vodka I wasn't used to. The Russians liked that. They hugged me. There'd been a little tension when I was the only one not drinking. But that was okay. We were past it.

They'd been *serious people* in the countries they fled, not flunkies, not landladies and waiters. I mean, even Mrs. SendInTheIdiots was probably a serious person in her own country and they were good, good people in the bargain. It was one of those great autumn days outside with the wind getting up and the leaves blowing around a little, not too sunny, not too gray. Windbreaker weather. It was that perfect moment between the afternoon and the evening and I thought that was probably what it was like to be a concert musician. There'd be these moments when you were playing Bizet with all these wonderful musicians, and you'd think, Why can't it stay like this? You know? I mean who could it hurt!

That was the last time I ever saw Rafael, and in some ways my most persistent memory of the afternoon is one I'd prefer to forget. Rafael tried a little too hard. He wanted you to see how he absorbed anything American. I mean, when dinner was finished, I went up to Rafael to hug him and thank him for including me, but he shook my hand instead. Rafael was a dear soul but he didn't know how to shake hands. His arm seemed to flap from the elbow once he released you, and it looked like he thought his hand was dirty now that you'd touched. And I knew as he released me just how much had changed after September eleventh, knew this for the first time really. You had to be born here now. Things were different.

Jon Tribble

Hooking Up

No obligation greater than no scars,
no bruises, no bite marks unless invited.

Equation of slick protection and skin
on skin long division where no ties

are binding, no cells dividing. Quick
entry or long, slow, sweet denial

till release from cuffs or velvet ropes,
performance nightly or daily or one

time only by request. The numbers
don't have to add up or still be

in service, and no one makes the coffee
or calls before the weekend.

Free to reach out for the next open hand
and the next, and after to wash away

nothing more than the last scent
clinging to your body like the finish

of a fine pinot or a ripple left too long
on the palate. Every body welcome,

or not, but it's catch and release,
and with so much coming and going,

does it matter what emptiness fills
and refills without communion,

without a chalice any more precious
than the next pitcher? This videogame

lovemaking keeps its own score,
and with all the faces and spaces

running out of memory, the reflection
in the screen continues to be alone—

if you can see anything at all.

Surrogates

My sister asks my wife to bear her child;
Or, rather, she asks me to ask for her.

And that—more than the phone calls she hasn't
returned in six months; more than my knowing

she, her husband, and her son will listen
to my voice wandering though the awkward

messages as I'm leaving them, my words
stumbling into electronic lockup

like a teetotaler blasted on Long
Island iced tea, lurching to an ugly

and confused mess; more even than her new
first name she decided her family—

especially our mother and father—
now must all use when writing or speaking

to her because she knew she never was
really just a ―Beth‖ or a ―Beth Ann‖ but

rather ―Elisabeth‖ spelled with an ―s‖
so the whistling sound can hiss from teeth and

lips like a radiator warning of
the predicaments of pressure—that choice

she has made to make me this messenger

tells me we have entered our adult lives

either not listening to one another
or not caring. I do not know how I

would feel if I thought my wife might ever
seriously entertain this notion,

how we would pass the nine months (if it took)—
my sister's egg, her second husband's seed,

their idea, their dream incubating as
we, a childless couple with no plans of

changing that situation, waited out
the weeks like a lease was winding down, games

of Scrabble and Boggle between doctor
visits, and then, when the day arrived, how

my wife would feel to lose this tenant, this
piece of not-her separating, turning

to its genetic nest now that the womb
no longer fed and warmed its days and nights?

But this is all academic: when I
lead up to the question whose answer I

already know, my wife's —Hell no‖ may not
be eloquent, but it is simple, it

is passionate, it is accurate, and
like a letter unanswered, a card or

gift unremarked, there is little room for
misinterpretation, no room for doubt.

Laundry

There was a time when I traveled
in the dark, sheer across 21st street -
pyjamas, padded slippers, quarters jangling
under my winter coat, as though a homeless person,
or a crazy, only to wash my sheets.

There was a time when I delivered my laundry
to a large Laundromatic drum, sat on a plastic chair
waiting for the cycle to finish, squeaky brown seat
upon bright orange linoleum. I wrote letters to you
on formica countertops as people were sorting their
whites from their darks.

There was a time when the operatics of soap suds
dying against a plastic porthole
distracted me from reading Great American Novels.
On Sundays I talked about the rain with the Chinese lady,
the one who had an endless supply of change in her jar.
New York was a hard place to live.

This is not New York. Today
our dirty linens have no duffel bag to contain them.
I carry them down carpeted stairs in bare feet.
The arms of our sweaters reach to each other,
your socks spin inside my socks.

Amy Schreibman Walter

Venice

In my loft bed, I told you I wanted
to see Venice in December,
see snow harden on gargoyle faces.

I wanted us to be somewhere other
than my room - its ladder, low ceilings.
I wanted a glimpse of a gondalier, shivering
as he led us into his boat.

I told you I wanted to be there
when the water had frozen, when
the tourists had given up looking.

You told me to bring a hat, you warned me
it might get cold when the wind lashes against my face.
You told me to wrap up warm if I should go.

I imagined the winter desertion
as romantic, a city sinking under its grace.

Contributors

Hobie Anthony writes prose and poetry in Portland, OR. A native of the South, adopted son of Chicago, and new NorthWesterner, he seeks to understand this America. He can be found or is forthcoming in such journals as The Los Angeles Review, Crate, Jersey Devil Press, R.kv.r.y., Wigleaf, Prime Number, and Soundzine, among others. He is now focused on putting together a new book.

Rusty Barnes' work has appeared in over a hundred fifty journals. He has published one book of flash fiction, *Breaking it Down*, 2007, sunnyoutside press. In early 2011, sunnyoutside will publish his collection of traditional fiction, *Mostly Redneck*. And last, his chapbook Redneck Poems is available for free on the internet.

J. Boyer teaches in the creative writing program at Arizona State University.

Wendy Taylor Carlisle is the author of two books of poetry, *Reading Berryman to the Dog (2000)* and *Discount Fireworks* (2008) and two chapbooks. She has lived in both Texas and Arkansas, therefore she holds dual citizenship. Read more about her, her dog, her and her work at wendytaylorcarlisle.com.

Portia Carryer is a graduate student at the University of Illinois, studying youth services librarianship. She has also infiltrated the creative writing department, where they let her take undergraduate poetry classes. She is originally from northern California, where she studied medieval history.

David Cozy is a writer and critic living in Japan. His work—fiction, criticism, or both—has appeared in *Harpers, Kyoto Journal, The Threepenny Review, The Review of Contemporary Fiction,* and elsewhere.

In addition, he reviews books regularly for *The Japan Times* and edits the review section of *Kyoto Journal.*

JP Dancing Bear lives near the Monterey Bay. His poems have appeared or are forthcoming in over a thousand publications. He is the author of several chapbooks, including *What Language,* winner of the 2002 Slipstream Prize. He is the author of three full-length poetry collections: *Billy Last Crow* (Turning Point, 2004); *Conflicted Light* (Salmon Poetry, 2008); *Inner Cities of Gulls* (Salmon Poetry, 2010); and *Family of Marsupial Centaurs (and other birthday poems)* coming out from Iris Press in late 2010. Dancing Bear's poems have been nominated ten times for Pushcart Prizes, for the Foreward Prize, and four times nominated for Best of the Web awards. In 2003, he was a finalist for the Alice Fay Di Castagnola Award from the Poetry Society of America for his manuscript *Gacela.* Bear's manuscript, *Lines Cast,* was a finalist in the 2008 National Poetry Series.

He is also the editor of *The American Poetry Journal.*

Lisbeth Davidow's essays have appeared in *Pilgrimage* and *Alligator Juniper.* Her essay, "Separation Anxiety," was a finalist in *Alligator Juniper's* 2008 National Creative Nonfiction contest and was nominated to be included in *Best of Creative Nonfiction, Volume 2.* She lives in Malibu, California with her husband.

Stephanie Dickinson has lived in Iowa, Texas, Louisiana and now in New York. Her novel *Half Girl,* winner of the Hackney Award (Birmingham-Southern) is published by Spuyten Duyvil. Her stories have been reprinted in *Best American Nonrequired Reading 2005, New Stories from the South, The Year's Best, 2008 and 2009. Road of Five Churches* and *Corn Goddess* are available from Rain Mountain Press. www.stephaniedickinson.net

Desiree Dighton has been a fiction finalist with *Glimmer Train Magazine* and *American Short Fiction.* This is her first published story. She currently lives in Raleigh, NC, where she is working on a novel.

Bryan Estes studies poetry among the corn and coal of the Middle West. He has read poems published in *Ploughshares, AGNI, Crazyhorse, The Kenyon Review*, and elsewhere.

Sheila Hageman is a multi-tasking mother of three. She received her MFA in Creative Writing from Hunter College, CUNY. She teaches Yoga, Creative Writing, Composition and Literature. She has been published in places like Salon, Conversely and Moxie. Check out her blog www.strippermom.blogspot.com.

Paul Kavanagh's writing credits include poetry and short stories in *Sleeping fish, Burnside Review, Fifth Wednesday Journal, Pen Pusher, Better Non Sequitur, Nano Fiction, Evergreen Review, Marginalia, Upstairs at Duroc, Mipoesias, 3am Magazine, Awkward Press, Monkeybicycle, Milk Magazine, American Drivel review, Trnsf* and soon to appear in *Flash Magazine, Riddle Fence, Mad Hatters Review* and *Anemone Sidecar.*

His book *The Killing of a Bank Manager* is published by Honest Publishing.

Grace Koong has just finished applying to MFA programs. These are her first published poems.

Jackson Lassiter lives and writes in Washington, DC. His work has appeared in over fifty anthologies and journals, most recently appeared in *Yalobusha Review, Gay City: Volume III,* and *Front Range Review.* In addition to his poetry, fiction, and creative non-fiction pieces, Lassiter is working on a gardening book and a novel set in Pensacola, Florida. Stay tuned, and contact him at LuckyJRL@hotmail.com.

Eleanor Levine's work has been published in *Fiction, The Denver Quarterly, Happy, Facets Magazine, The Toronto Quarterly*, and other publications and anthologies. She received an MFA in Creative Writing from Hollins University in 2007, and is currently a copy editor in New Jersey and lives in Philadelphia. She adores Philip Roth and her dog, Virginia Woolf.

John C. Mannone, nominated three times for the Pushcart Prize in Poetry and once for the Rhysling Poetry Award, has over 150 poems/fiction published in literary and speculative fiction journals, including *Lucid Rhythms*, *The Linnet's Wings*, *Skive*, *Mobius* and *Pirene's Fountain*. He's on the poetry faculty for *To Write Well* and is the poetry editor for *Silver Blade*. When not writing, he researches astrophysics and volunteers as a NASA/JPL Solar System Ambassador. Visit his site, The Art of Poetry, at http://jcmannone.wordpress.com.

Michael Meyerhofer's third book, *Damnatio Memoriae*, won the Brick Road Poetry Book Contest. His previous books are *Blue Collar Eulogies* (Steel Toe Books) and *Leaving Iowa* (winner of the Liam Rector First Book Award). He has also won five chapbook prizes. His work has appeared in *Ploughshares*, *North American Review*, *Arts & Letters*, *River Styx*, *Quick Fiction* and other journals, and can be read online at www.troublewithhammers.com.

Dustin J. Monk spends a lot of time on the road, writing and playing bass. He is a recent graduate of the Clarion Writers' Workshop in San Diego. He can be found at http://spiralzine.blogspot.com.

Kate Ristow holds an MFA from the University of Montana. Currently she lives and teaches in Ketchum, Idaho.

Amy Schreibman Walter was born in Florida. She lives in London, where she studies at the Faber Poetry Academy. Her poems are published or forthcoming in magazines including *The Battered Suitcase*, *Neon* and *The Meadowland Review*. She is at work on her first pamphlet of poems.

Jared Yates Sexton lives in Indiana, where he teaches writing at Ball State University. He is a Contributing Editor at *BULL* and his collection of stories, *Just Listen*, was recently named a finalist for the New American Fiction Prize. His work has appeared in magazines and journals around the world.

Jon Tribble's poems have appeared in the anthologies *Surreal South*, *Two Weeks*, and *Where We Live: Illinois Poets*, in print in the *Southeast Review*, *Black Zinnias*, and *Southern Indiana Review*, and online at *Caper Literary Journal*. He teaches at Southern Illinois University Carbondale, where he is the managing editor of *Crab Orchard Review* and the series editor of the Crab Orchard Award Series in Poetry published by SIU Press.